A Christmas Carol

BASED ON THE BOOK BY
CHARLES DICKENS

By Michael Paller

D1553870

SAMUEL FRENCH, INC.
45 WEST 25TH STREET   NEW YORK 10010
7623 SUNSET BOULEVARD HOLLYWOOD 90046
LONDON   TORONTO

A CHRISTMAS CAROL was originally produced by Center Repertory Theatre of Cleveland. The production was directed by Thomas Q. Fulton, Jr., with sets and lighting designed by James Merrill Stone and costumes designed by Mark Passerell. Musical supervisor was Michael Griffith. The production opened December 8th, 1978, with the following cast:

MARK LEMON .... *Robert Snook*

FREDERICK DICKENS .... *Bradley Boyer*

CLARKSON STANFIELD .... *David Willis*

HELEN HOGARTH .... *Maureen Pedala*

CHARLEY DICKENS .... *Jeff Granger*

MRS. STANFIELD .... *Mary Ann Nagel*

CATHERINE DICKENS .... *Margaret Heffernan*

CHARLES DICKENS .... *Thomas Q. Fulton, Jr.*

JOHN FORSTER .... *Gary Bodiford*

CAST OF CHARACTERS
(in order of appearance)

CHARLES DICKENS—Tall, slim, seldom standing still; a dynamo of energy with a mesmerizing voice. In his early thirties, he is already near the height of his powers.

THE CHILD—Ten years old. Dressed in shades of grey and black.

MARK LEMON—Editor of "Punch" magazine, the humorous weekly. He is advancing toward middle age and corpulence.

FREDERICK DICKENS—The younger brother of CHARLES DICKENS. Twenty-three, he is something of a ne'er-do-well, the charming variety.

CLARKSON STANFIELD—The painter. About thirty-two, there is a quality about him that is, at once, mischievous yet gentle.

HELEN HOGARTH—The ten-year old niece of CHARLES DICKENS.

CHARLEY DICKENS—CHARLES DICKENS' son, also about ten.

MRS. STANFIELD—Wife of STANFIELD. In her early thirties, she is small and delicately featured, with the most amazing pair of dancing eyes.

CATHERINE DICKENS—Wife of CHARLES DICKENS. She is also in her late twenties or early thirties. A taller woman than MRS. STANFIELD, her beauty is of a sturdier sort.

JOHN FORSTER—DICKENS' closest friend and advisor. Also in his thirties, he is in many ways the opposite of DICKENS: Though given to occasional fits of joviality, he is more by nature gruff and taciturn.

The time is Christmas Eve, 1843.
The place is the attic of the home of Charles Dickens in London.

WHO PLAYS WHO

DICKENS—SCROOGE

CHARLEY—A CAROLLER, YOUNG EBENEZER, A LITTLE FEZZIWIG, TINY TIM, THE BOY

HELEN—A CAROLLER, FAN, A LITTLE FEZZIWIG, BELINDA CRATCHIT

STANFIELD—BOB CRATCHIT, THE GHOST OF CHRISTMAS PAST, TOPPER, THE THIN MAN, THE UNDERTAKER

MRS. STANFIELD—BELLE, MARTHA CRATCHIT, MRS. FRED'S SISTER, THE CHARWOMAN

CATHERINE DICKENS—MRS. FEZZIWIG, MRS. CRATCHIT, MRS. FRED, MRS. DILBER

FREDERICK DICKENS—FRED, YOUNG SCROOGE, PETER CRATCHIT, GHOST OF CHRISTMAS YET TO COME (I), OLD JOE

JOHN FORSTER—SECOND PORTLY GENTLEMAN, GHOST OF JACOB MARLEY, DICK WILKINS, GHOST OF CHRIST-MAS PRESENT, MAN WITH THE HANDKERCHIEF, GHOST OF CHRISTMAS YET TO COME (II)

MARK LEMON—FIRST PORTLY GENTLEMAN, FEZZIWIG, FAT MAN, MAN ON THE BED

THE CHILD

A Christmas Carol

PROLOGUE

The set has three levels. The first level, which in terms of playing space, is the largest; the second, which is about six or so inches higher, is smaller in area; the third is a round turret, with steps leading down to the second level. The room is a third story attic. It is as clean as any other room in the house, as its owner often spends his day there. The main entrance to the room is a door on the turret. Through this door one may enter from the lower floors of the house. The turret is Up Left. Up Right, in the Right wall, is a smaller door to a smaller storage room. Just down of this door is a fireplace with fire irons and a wood box. In the center of the rear wall is a large window, and a window seat which opens up for storage. Right of the window, set into the wall, are bookshelves. Downstage, on the first level, is a writing desk and chair. To the Right, also Downstage, is a couch, or chaise longue. Downstage of the chaise longue, on the edge of the stage, is a window which we cannot see. Center, on the second level, is a large, humpbacked trunk. There are a few other chairs, scattered about. A large gas lamp hangs from the ceiling over the center of the room; hurricane lamps and candles are on brackets on the walls and on the mantle; also there is a candle and candlestick on the writing desk. On the turret wall is a set of bells connected to the floors below for communication purposes (and can be rung Offstage). Atop the room are rafters, through which we can see the sky. A lecturn stands to the Left of the turret.

The house belongs to one CHARLES DICKENS. *It is noon, December 24th, 1843, in London.*

CHARLES DICKENS, *a tall, powerfully built man with a moustache, and a beard on his chin (which, I confess, he did not have in 1843), sits at his desk, trying to write. He is disturbed by the sounds of carollers' voices, which float into the room through the window, which is slightly ajar. Angered by the distraction, he throws down his pen, goes to the window, and shuts it. He returns to the desk, picks up his pen, and writes one more word.*

DICKENS. (*Writing.*) "Autobiography." (*He puts down the pen, and reads what he's written this morning.*) These, then are the facts. When I was ten, my father was declared a bankrupt, and was incarcerated in Marshalsea, the debtors' prison. His creditors determined that some member of our family had to earn wages. So, I was taken away, and placed in a damp, lightless factory, where they manufactured bootblacking. For twelve hours a day, I pasted labels on blacking jars. I was diligent in my work, and tried not to hear the incessant scurry beneath the floorboards. Or I would close my eyes, and pretend that it was rain on the window, and that I was safely home in bed. But when the noises began running squealing between my legs, even an imagination as resolute as mine could not make of them anything but what they were. (*He crosses out the next few words, and continues.*) Some days, the owner would set me in a large window, and people would stop to admire the little man at work. This would usually occur around midday, when the streets were full. Later, the owner—a cousin of mine—would happily report that my performance was responsible for the immediate and large purchases made by the lunch hour crowds. To a boy whose world was bound by sunlight and a lazy blue river, this descent into meanness and filth seemed like the end of life. My companions were street urchins, who had little sympathy for a boy who knew how to read—and liked to. I was totally friendless. I spoke to no one, except at night, when I visited my father in his cell. I wanted him to know the misery of my existence . . . (*He pauses, thinking how to procede. It should be mentioned that, although the time of day is noon, the room is dark. Only those parts of the room that are currently in play are lit. As other parts of the room come into play, they, too, are lit. During the PROLOGUE, the room is never bright. At present, all we see is* DICKENS *at his desk. Now, from out of the darkness, comes a small hand reaching across the desk. We begin to see that it belongs to a* CHILD *about ten years old.* THE CHILD *takes the paper* DICKENS *has been reading from, and crumples it. He—for it is a boy, dressed in simple shirt and pants of a poor London boy of the 1820's—crosses to the fireplace and tosses the paper in. He turns and faces* DICKENS.) You are a most disagreeable child.

THE CHILD. (*Shrugging his shoulders.*) Yes.

DICKENS. Listen. I wrote this this morning. (*He takes another sheet of paper and begins to read aloud. As he does,* THE CHILD *wanders Upstage, takes some books from the shelves, riffles through the pages, and drops them on the floor. His attention is then drawn to the trunk. He crosses to it, opens it, and begins examining its contents.*) I am a grown man. Or as grown a man as any writer comes to be. But more and more, I find that I must answer to the whims of a little boy. Now and then he comes to me during the day as I work. (*He pauses, as a book hits the floor.*) Listen. This is about you. (*He goes back to the manuscript.*) Most of the time, he comes for me at night. And though I am a man and he is only a boy, he compels me, by some power, to follow him. He guides me down ill-lit, constricted streets, until I can smell the river. I know where he is leading me, and I stop, as a dark structure rears up out of the night. "No!" I say. "I would follow you if I could, but I haven't the power.'' I turn and flee, back up the twisted lanes, up away from the river. I push my way through a noisy crowd, and see the faces of friends and relations long dead. I shout to them, but they have no consciousness of me. I'm carried along until I find myself in a mean little street in the Camdentown slum. Before me is a tumbledown pawnshop. Three grotesque creatures are bickering with the proprietor— (*He stops because* THE CHILD *is now banging loudly on a toy drum he has taken from the trunk.* DICKENS *stands.* THE CHILD *stops his banging. A pause, while their eyes meet.* DICKENS *sighs, crumples the paper, and tosses it to* THE CHILD, *who takes it to the fireplace and throws it in.*) I'm trying to reach an accomodation. Look. (*He crosses to the chaise longue and takes from under it an old box. He opens it.*) I found these last night, rummaging about. (*From the box, he takes some old toys: a wooden soldier whose arms and legs move with the pull of a string; a tumbler who rolls about; a frog made of Plaster-of-Paris.*) Don't you recognize them?

THE CHILD. (*Crossing to the desk, he sits and looks through a stack of manuscript.*) No.

DICKENS. They're Christmas toys, you old goat. For all his faults, John Dickens knew how to choose a Christmas gift. Come see. (*He offers one to* THE CHILD.) They're yours, too.

THE CHILD. (*Reading from a page of manuscript.*) ''Despite our poverty, the spirit of Christmas filled our poor house like a living giant.'' (*He crumples the paper.*)

DICKENS. (*Trying not to be annoyed.*) I can't seem to come up with anything that pleases you. (THE CHILD *crosses to the fireplace and throws the paper in.*) Can't we be at peace? It doesn't become a man to war with children. (*He crosses to* THE CHILD, *who counters by crossing back to the desk.*)

THE CHILD. They're a trap.

DICKENS. What?

THE CHILD. The toys.

DICKENS. No they're not. (*A pause.*) Yes they are. Of sorts. I simply want to make you a part of me again. (*He holds out his hand.*) Won't you come to me?

THE CHILD. No.

DICKENS. What would you like me to do?

THE CHILD. (*Thinking.*) Stand on your head.

DICKENS. I will not stand on my head.

THE CHILD. Sing a Christmas song, then.

DICKENS. (*Not pleased.*) Very well. (*He sings the first few lines of "Come, All Ye Faithful," until* THE CHILD *begins to laugh.*) This is ridiculous. (THE CHILD *breaks the point off a quill. Then, he breaks another.*) It isn't enough that you haunt me, is it? (THE CHILD *jumps from the chair and crosses to the window seat. He looks out the window.*) You simply must defy me, as well. (*No response from* THE CHILD.) I know that I've not always used you well, that I've blamed you for faults which are my own. And I've behaved bitterly toward you. I admit that, too. But not any more.

THE CHILD. (*Looking out the window.*) There's a man with a goose downstairs.

DICKENS. Yes, we're having a Christmas Eve party tonight.

THE CHILD. He has another goose.

DICKENS. A sure sign that Mark Lemon will be here. And that's one more reason why I wish you'd be more . . . attentive. (*From a desk drawer he takes a stack of bills.*) Goose is not inexpensive. Neither is clothing. Nor coal. Nor paper. Nor . . . quills. And I can't get any amount of work done with you laying so unproductively on every thought.

THE CHILD. (*Unimpressed, he crosses to the trunk, and takes from it a violin and bow.*) Do you think he has to work tonight?

DICKENS. Who?

THE CHILD. The goose man.

DICKENS. Probably.

THE CHILD. Must have a nasty boss, making him work on Christmas Eve.

DICKENS. Don't play with that. (*He takes the instrument from* THE CHILD. *On second thought, he hands it back.*) The fact that I've resorted to putting it all down on paper says something. (*Leafing through the manuscript.*)

THE CHILD. (*Plucking the strings and drawing the bow across them.*) I wanted to take music lessons.

DICKENS. Yes, it would have been nice. (*Looking at a particular page.*) Did you know about the girl I was in love with when I was eighteen?

THE CHILD. No.

DICKENS. She was quite pretty. Yes, she was. Of course, she was very frivolous, too, but—

THE CHILD. (*Takes a crutch from the trunk, and with great energy, hops across the floor.*) Who am I?

DICKENS. I don't know.

THE CHILD. Guess.

DICKENS. The Queen's Color Guard.

THE CHILD. No.

DICKENS. I give up.

THE CHILD. The boy with the crutch.

DICKENS. Ah. Well, you're much too clever for me.

THE CHILD. From the factory. The boy with the crutch.

DICKENS. What boy with a crutch? I don't remember anyone like that.

THE CHILD. That's because there wasn't any.

DICKENS. Of course there wasn't. (*But he's intrigued.*) But what if there were? What if there were a boy with a crutch? Would he in fact be able to work? His family would have to be in a bad situation to even consider it. What about his brothers and sisters? (THE CHILD *goes to the window and opens it. Again, the sound of the carollers wafts in. The stage begins to darken, until all we see is* DICKENS.) They'd have to put in long hours at some menial labor to bring home even five and sixpence weekly. And the father? A laborer, or a clerk, perhaps . . . with an old pinchfist of an employer opposed on principle to paying a living wage . . . (*He turns and looks for* THE CHILD, *who has vanished in the darkness.*) What the devil . . . (*Back to the new thought.*) And what if this employer had a partner . . . (*The lights fade as he continues to speak.*)

ACT ONE

Christmas Eve. The room is dark, except for a shaft of moonlight shining through the window. The singing voices have grown louder; they are now coming from downstairs. There is a burst of laughter, followed by renewed singing. A scrambling, huffing, and puffing is heard on the stairs, and MARK LEMON *bursts into the room, as if squeezed out of the narrow stairway.* LEMON *is close to middle age, balding on top but well-whiskered on the sides, and given to corpulence. There is a great deal of child about him still, as befits the first editor of "Punch," the humor magazine. The Dickens family has nicknamed this sleek, round gentleman "Uncle Porpoise."*

Currently, he is something other than jovial. He's just been chased up two flights of stairs, the last considerably narrower than he. He pauses on the turret, and after a moment, spies a candle on DICKENS' *desk. He gropes his way toward it, barking his shins on the trunk.*

LEMON. Merry Christmas indeed, Charles Dickens! (*Limping his way to the desk, he strikes a match and lights the candle.*) If our Savior had known we would be celebrating his eighteen hundred and forty-third birthday in such a fasion, he'd have returned and put an end to things long ago. (*Seeing the trunk, and sitting on it.*) It was you who confounded my shins, was it?

(*There is another clamor on the steps, singing and laughing.* FREDERICK DICKENS, *the 23 year-old ne'er-do-well brother of* CHARLES, *enters, carrying* CHARLEY, DICKENS' *young son on his shoulders. He is followed*

14

by the artist CLARKSON STANFIELD, *who is 32, and bearing* DICKENS' *niece,* HELEN HOGARTH, *on his shoulders.* FREDERICK *is long and lanky, with sandy red hair.* STANFIELD *is a bit shorter, wiry, and dark-haired. The children have draped their mounts with much Christmas trimming.* HELEN *also carries a box of it. As they speak, the four of them drape the room in garlands, wreaths, pine cones, etc.)*

FREDERICK. Heigh-ho, Uncle Porpoise!

STANFIELD. I've never seen any man run so.

FREDERICK. Never seen so large a man run so, you mean.

STANFIELD. (*Putting* HELEN *down.*) Off you go, about your work.

LEMON. Work?

HELEN. Uncle Boz told us to trim the room like a tree.

CHARLEY. "Do it up proper," he said, "or I'll show you how."

LEMON. He's gone mad.

(HELEN *and* CHARLEY, *who is off* FREDERICK's *shoulders at this point, continue dressing up the room.*)

FREDERICK. He *is* excited.

STANFIELD. You excited him, Mark Lemon.

CHARLEY. (*Correcting him.*) "Uncle Porpoise!"

LEMON. (*Taking hard candy from a vest pocket, and tossing some to the children.*) I only suggested he tell us a Christmas story. And, as it is Christmas Eve, I think that's a thoroughly proper and reasonable request. Next thing I know, he's chasing me about with a broomstick, bellowing, "Up the stairs, to the attic with you!"

STANFIELD. You cut quite a figure—and quite a path, too. You tumbled every vase in the vicinity, I think.

FREDERICK. The retreat you beat up those stairs was hilarious—as funny as anything I've seen in your magazine for years. But I think you've inflicted grave injury on that last flight of stairs. They were groaning in considerable pain when we came up. (*The last candle is lit at this point.*)

LEMON. Christmas has driven him mad. The most famous writer in England—I think we're entitled to a story.

STANFIELD. He absolutely refuses.

FREDERICK. He is adamant.

STANFIELD. He's got something up his sleeve, the old magician.

LEMON. The old murderer, you mean. I nearly broke my legs over this trunk.

FREDERICK. Oh, that's the theatrical trunk. For the costumes, and so on. You've never seen our theatricals, have you, Uncle Porpoise? Stanny here paints the scenery, you know—and acts, as well.

STANFIELD. They're a smashing piece of fun. Dickens chooses the plays, rehearses us night and day for a month, and we take 'em out for charity. We've all of us done 'em. Even the children.

FREDERICK. Sometimes they're the best of us all. It's their imaginations, I think.

HELEN. No it's not. It's our talent.

FREDERICK. That modest estimation proves she's a Dickens, if only by marriage. Forster does 'em, too.

LEMON. No. Forster? I can't imagine a man with the social amenities of a porcupine painting his face and frisking across a stage. He kills daisies with a stare. It's his hobby, you know.

FREDERICK. We've raised hundreds for the childrens' hospitals.

LEMON. That trunk very nearly landed me in hospital.

FREDERICK. You should see him work. His energy is extraordinary. Between driving us like slaves and taking the principle role himself, one would swear he's possessed by demons.

DICKENS. (*Off.*) Up, up with you!

LEMON. Good God, he's driving the women up, too!

(CATHERINE *and* MRS. STANFIELD *enter.* CATHERINE, *a handsome woman in her early thirties, is a sturdy Victorian mother.* MRS. STANFIELD *is bubbling innocence personified.* CATHERINE *is maneuvering a large brimming punch bowl, while* MRS. STANFIELD *carries a tray of glasses.* LEMON *immediately goes to the aid of* CATHERINE, *while* FREDERICK *assists* MRS. STANFIELD. STANFIELD *is looking through the contents of the trunk.*)

MRS. STANFIELD. (*Out of breath.*) I don't know how we've done it, but we haven't spilled a drop.

CATHERINE. He'd have our heads if we did. He insists we have the punch.

FREDERICK. Bravo, ladies, remarkable feat! (*Having helped* MRS. STANFIELD, *he exits into the small room Off Right, for a reconnaissance.*)

MRS. STANFIELD. I think it's an accomplishment, to be chased 'round a table and up two flights of stairs carrying a full bowl of punch, and not spilling a drop. What could he be thinking?

FREDERICK. (*Reentering with a horse collar connected to several chains.*) Something outrageous, I'm quite confident.

LEMON. My goodness, he takes this slave business seriously, doesn't he?

FREDERICK. (*Putting the collar on* LEMON.) Yes, and I think it's just your size, too.

LEMON. (*Quickly evading the collar.*) Fortunately, my dear Frederick—and, as you would be the first to point out—these days, I can find very little that *is* my size.

CATHERINE. Well, if this is any indication, I'm certain

we'll need to fortify ourselves for whatever it is he has in mind. Have some punch.

STANFIELD. (*Taking the violin and bow from the trunk.*) Look at this, my dear. A serenade!

MRS. STANFIELD. Oh, Stanny. Please not a seranade.

STANFIELD. (*Tuning.*) And why not? I'm quite handy with a fiddle and bow.

MRS. STANFIELD. (*She playfully takes the bow from him. As she speaks,* STANFIELD *makes a valiant attempt to regain it.*) I know several cats who would disagree. (*To the others.*) Stanny played the violin for a week beneath my window before I agreed to marry him, and only under the strictest condition that he give up music and swear fidelity to his artist's brush.

STANFIELD. (*Still chasing after the bow.*) Nonsense. We agreed only that I not play beneath your window, and I haven't. (*He's got it back.*) As for the alley cats—well, they obviously recognized in the strings of my instrument a long lost cousin, and were understandably shaken. (*He turns his back on* MRS. STANFIELD, *and announces:*) Now then, ladies and gents, ''The Christmas Child.'' (*He raises his bow to the violin. As he's about to strike the first note,* MRS. STANFIELD *tickles him from behind. This surprise attack propels him in the direction of* CATHERINE, *and he now has his back to her.*) Narrow-minded critic! (CATHERINE *covers his eyes from behind.*) I say! Everything's gone dark! (*He leaps onto the chaise longue.*) Muses protect me! All the marshalled forces of Christendom shall not prevent me from being heard! Ladies and gents, ''The Christmas Child!'' (*He raises the bow and is about to strike the first note when a loud crash is heard downstairs.*)

LEMON. Good heavens, what is that man up to?

CHARLEY. (*Meaning the decorations.*) There, Uncle Porpoise. Does it look like Christmas?

LEMON. It's superb, Charley. All it lacks is a tree.

DICKENS. (*Beginning Off, we hear deep, mysterious tones. Midway through the verse, he enters. Or, rather, some being, possibly human, piled high with household items, wrapped Christmas gifts, and a coat rack, festooned with various bits of costume, enters. One prominent appendage is a large branch cut from a Christmas tree and stuck, with some earth, in a pot. He has a black, hooded robe over his clothes.*)
''We three kings of Orient are
bearing gifts we've travelled afar.
Field and fountain,
moor and mountain,
following yonder star.''
    (*He sets down the coat rack, and points a finger at* CHARLEY.)
Child, which way to the East?
    LEMON. Good God.
    CATHERINE. What have you done to the tree, Charles?
    DICKENS. It insisted I bring some of it upstairs. ''Take a bough!'' it said! ''I don't want to be left out. I've plenty more and won't miss it a minute. You'll have it back in me by Christmas morning, and I'll never know the difference!''
    FREDERICK. What is all this?
    DICKENS. I've seen a vision. A miser's bed . . . (*From his collection he pulls a sheet, and throws it onto the couch, practically covering* LEMON.)
    LEMON. I say!
    DICKENS. . . . a boy with a crutch . . . (*He tosses* CHARLEY *the crutch.*)
    STANFIELD. He busted the broomstick!
    DICKENS. . . . a man wrapped in chains! Stunning, brilliant idea! (*He examines the faces in the room.*) The one who's missing will be here directly. And won't he be in a temper! (*Crossing to the downstage window, gazing out.*) The night is folding itself around us. Come look! The

moonlight fades as the fog slides in. It's freezing, thawing, snivelling. The pavement's greasy with the damp; nothing can stand in the street, and nobody can quite fall.

LEMON. A good night to be in doors. By a fire. In the parlour.

DICKENS. I'd quite forgotten. I apologize. Fred! By all means, a fire!

FREDERICK. Right! (FREDERICK *builds a fire in the fireplace.*)

DICKENS. We can't very well have a Christmas story without a fire blazing.

MRS. STANFIELD. So it *is* a story.

CATHERINE. You needn't put us through all of this for the sake of a story. You could have told it as easily in the parlour.

STANFIELD. No, don't be silly. I have it. He wants to tell it here, where he writes—to be "inspired" by the atmosphere.

(*A general clamor, as they debate the necessity of moving the entire party upstairs.*)

DICKENS. Peace, peace! This is Christmas Eve. It's my work telling stories. Surely you don't suggest a man work upon Christmas Eve? No, I've something else in mind. (*The bells on the wall jangle.*) He's here—my man in chains. I want everyone to greet him with a hearty "Merry Christmas, John!" But first, be prepared for a blow, batten down the hatches! Hide! (*They do so. Some exit into the room Off Right,* STANFIELD *lifts* HELEN *into the trunk and shuts the lid, one hides behind the chaise.* LEMON *stays where he is, on the chaise.*) Submerge yourself, Uncle Porpoise!

(LEMON *covers himself with the blanket.* DICKENS *turns down the gas lamp, and hides by the corner of the stairway, the hood of the cloak draped over his head. A pause. A sound of footsteps on the stairs.* JOHN FORSTER *enters. He is* DICKENS' *closest friend, a literary critic and editor whose temper is infamous. For* FORSTER, *it is an effort to look anything but grim and disagreeable. He is irritated and somewhat confused, for upon arrival he has been told by the maid that the party has been moved to the attic. He pauses on the turret, letting his eyes adjust to the darkness.*)

FORSTER. Hello? Dickens? (*He comes down the stairs, and straight down front.* DICKENS *follows from behind, and points a cloaked arm at* FORSTER.) Anybody here?

DICKENS. (*Deeply, mysteriously.*) Merry Christmas, John. (FORSTER *jumps in fright, as* EVERYONE *bursts into view with:*)

EVERYONE. Merry Christmas, John!

FORSTER. (*To* DICKENS.) You lunatic. An explanation at once.

DICKENS. (*Putting the gas lamp back on.*) Gentle Forster, meek and mild! Merry Christmas!

HELEN. (*Standing in the trunk.*) I don't see any chains.

FORSTER. Chains? What's she talking about?

DICKENS. Ladies and gentlemen, my good, most understanding friend, Mister John Forster. You know everyone, Forster? I don't believe you've met my niece, Helen.

FORSTER. No. (*Children do not impress him.*) Merry Christmas.

CATHERINE. (*Holding out her hand.*) Merry Christmas, John.

FORSTER. (*Kissing it.*) Yes, yes. Now, will you explain why we're celebrating this auspicious night in such an unorthodox, uncomfortable, and odious little room?

STANFIELD. It's simple. Uncle Porpoise here suggested that Dickens tell us a Christmas tale, and instead of sitting us round the fire, he's herded us all upstairs.

FORSTER. You asked Dickens to tell a story? And he refused? Don't stand there, man, fetch a doctor. He's unmistakably ill.

DICKENS. (*Enjoying it all.*) No, no; I'm as healthy as the good day itself. And I'd be as glad of a Christmas story as you'd be. But if there's a worse sin than working upon Christmas Eve, it's one man doing all the work while the rest sink back and savor his industry. No. If we're to have a story, let us each take a part in its telling. Everything we need for a tale of Christmas is in this room. (*He throws open the trunk.*) The costumes and properties of Dickens' Theatricals! (*He takes off the cloak.*)

FREDERICK. I say, this could be fun.

DICKENS. It will be glorious. Place yourselves in my hands. We'll bring forth the most marvelous of Christmas spirits. Now, for the roles . . .

FORSTER. Just a moment here, friend Dickens. We're going to tell a Christmas story?

DICKENS. We're going to perform a Christmas story, yes, John.

FORSTER. Are there ghosts and such things in this story?

DICKENS. Most assuredly. What's a Christmas story without them?

FORSTER. And we, respectable adults, are going to glide about, pretending to be these ghosts, which are strictly the products of over-fertile imaginations?

DICKENS. Yes, again, John. (*A pause.*)

FORSTER. Do I get to play 'em?

DICKENS. My entire plan rests on the very assumption that you'll play a number of ghosts.

FORSTER. Good. Otherwise, I'd not participate. But, as it stands—I'll do it. (*There's a boy in* FORSTER, *too.*) And I'll act the devil out of all of you!

DICKENS. Bravo! Now, the roles. (*As he makes the assignments,* DICKENS *gives each person a prop, or an article of clothing which they will use in some way in some point—or in various points—of the story. Tied to each*

item—all of which are on the coat rack except for the ring—is a scroll on which DICKENS *has written a brief description of each of the first characters they will play. To* CHARLEY, *a cap. To* HELEN, *a shawl. To* CATHERINE, *a bonnet, with a ragged grey wig attached. To* STANFIELD, *a quill pen. To* FREDERICK, *a top hat. To* MRS. STANFIELD, *a gold ring which he takes from his vest pocket. To* LEMON, *a welsh wig. To* FORSTER, *a large, distinctive handkerchief.*)
To Charley, the very young gentlemen, beginning with a caroller. To Helen, the very young ladies, also beginning with a caroller. Now, you two pick a carol you both know—a good one, too. As for you, Stanny, to you fall the young, hardworking men—a role to which you're well accustomed, beginning with a clerk called Cratchit. Frederick, to you, a mixture of the dandies and the men who are determined to get ahead and accomplish great things in the world—a role to which you are thoroughly unaccustomed. Begin with a nephew named, of all names, Fred. For you, my dear Catherine, the matrons and the mothers—the latter position you fill so well, and are acquainted with through experience, though the former will demand imagination on your part. Your first assignment is a creature known as Mrs. Fezziwig. As for you, Mrs. Stanfield, all the young and available ladies; for Uncle Porpoise, those roles which are the most well-rounded; and for you, Forster, all that's left—including a ghost or two. Within these bounds, feel free to play whomever and whatever you like. I shan't be annoyed if you stretch or exchange assignments on occasion, so long as you act for the sake of the story.

(*During this speech, the following activities occur:* STAN-FIELD *removes his coat and hangs it on the coat rack, which is carried back up to the turret.* CATHERINE *and* MRS. STANFIELD *move the lectern to the landing of the turret, and* FREDERICK *places a high stool behind it. An ink pot is taken from the trunk and is placed on*

*the lecturn, along with some paper—or, the ink pot
may already be fastened onto the lecturn. DICKENS
takes a few small money sacks and a large ledger from
the trunk, and puts them on the desk. A quill, an ink-
pot, and the candlestick are already there.*)

DICKENS. Make use of the items I've given you; carry
them through the entire tale, giving a unity to our work.
Use whatever you like in this room: use the costumes, use
the furniture. Use each other. Confer, if you like. Bear in
mind one thing only: Marley is dead. There is no doubt
whatever about that. This must be distinctly understood,
or nothing wonderful will come of the story we are about to
create. Marley is dead as a doornail. Mind, I don't mean
to say that I know, of my own knowledge, what there is
particularly dead about a doornail. I might have been in-
clined to regard a coffin nail as the deadest piece of iron-
mongery in the trade. But, the wisdom of our ancestors
is in the simile, and my unhallowed hands shall not disturb
it. You will therefore permit me to repeat, emphatically,
that Marley is dead as a doornail. (*With FORSTER's aid,
he moves the desk Down Center of the second level, and
places one chair behind it, and one chair to its Left.*)
Scrooge knew he was dead? Of course he did. How could it
be otherwise? Scrooge and he were partners, for I don't
know how many years. (*He and FORSTER shake hands.
FORSTER then turns to exit through the door, Right.*)
Scrooge was his sole executor, his sole administrator, his
sole assign, his sole residuary legatee, his sole friend,
and his sole mourner. (FORSTER *pauses at the door.*) And
even Scrooge was not so terribly cut up by the sad event.
Being an excellent man of business, on the very day of the
funeral, he solemnized the occasion with an undoubted bar-
gain. Scrooge never painted out old Marley's name.
There it stood, years afterward, above the warehouse door:

Scrooge and Marley. (FORSTER *exits.* DICKENS *puts on a coat, which has been hanging on the back of the desk chair, and turns down the gas lamp, darkening the room.*) Once upon a time—of all good days in the year, on Christmas Eve—old Scrooge sat busy in his counting house. It was cold, bleak, biting weather. The city clocks had only just gone three, but it was quite dark already; it had not been light all day. The fog came pouring in at every chink and keyhole. (*He takes a small make-up box from a drawer. As speaks, he applies some paint to his face, a false nose, a grey wig, and a pair of wire-rimmed spectacles.*) Oh, but he was a tightfisted hand at the grindstone, Scrooge! A squeezing, wrenching, grasping, scraping, clutching, covetous old sinner! Hard and sharp as flint, from which no steel had ever struck out generous fire. The cold within him froze his old features, nipped his pointed nose, shrivelled his cheek, stiffened his gait; made his eyes red, his thin lips blue, and spoke out shrewdly in his grating voice. A frosty rime was on his head, his eyebrows, and his wiry chin. He carried his own low temperature always about with him. He iced his office in the dog days, and he didn't thaw it one degree at Christmas.

(*He is now* SCROOGE. *Everyone has left the stage but* SCROOGE *and* BOB CRATCHIT, *who is busily writing at his desk on the turret, and trying not to notice the cold. A pause.* FREDERICK, *as nephew* FRED, *bursts into the room, from Up Right.*)

FRED. (*Tossing a small gift—a candy cane, or a piece of fruit, perhaps—to* CRATCHIT.) A merry Christmas, uncle! God save you!

SCROOGE. (*Annoyed at the intrusion, he looks up for a moment, but not at* FRED. *Then, back to work.*) Bah. Humbug.

FRED. Christmas a humbug, uncle? You don't mean that, I'm sure.

SCROOGE. I do. "Merry Christmas." What right have you to be merry? What reason have you? You're poor enough.

FRED. Come then, what right have you to be dismal? You're rich enough.

SCROOGE. What's Christmas time to you but a time for paying bills without money? A time for finding yourself a year older but not an hour richer; a time for balancing your books and having every item in 'em presented dead against you. Bah. Humbug!

FRED. Don't be cross, uncle.

SCROOGE. What else can I be when I live in such a world of fools as this? Merry Christmas! Out upon merry Christmas! If I could work my will, every idiot who goes about with "Merry Christmas" on his lips should be boiled with his own pudding, and buried with a stake of holly through his heart. He should!

FRED. Uncle!

SCROOGE. (*Getting up from his desk with a few money bags and crossing to a small safe—a hinged floorboard.*) Nephew! Keep Christmas in your own way, and let me keep it in mine.

FRED. Keep it? But you don't keep it.

SCROOGE. Let me leave it alone, then. Much good may it do you. Much good it has ever done you.

FRED. There are many things from which I have derived good by which I have not profited, I dare say—Christmas among them. It's the only time I know of when men and women open their shut-up hearts and think of less fortunate people as if they really were fellow-passengers to the grave, and not another race of creatures. And therefore, uncle, though it has never put a scrap of gold or silver in my pocket, I believe that it has done me good, and I say God bless it!

(*He puts a stick of wood on the fire.* CRATCHIT *bursts into applause at the end of the speech.*)

SCROOGE. (*Standing. To* CRATCHIT.) Let me hear another sound from you, and you'll keep your Christmas by losing your situation. (*To* FRED.) You're quite a powerful speaker, sir. I wonder you don't go into Parliament.

FRED. Don't be angry, uncle. Come dine with us tomorrow

SCROOGE. (*Back at his desk.*) I'll dine with the devil first.

FRED. But why, uncle?

SCROOGE. Why did you get married?

FRED. Because I fell in love.

SCROOGE. (*As if that were the only thing in the world more ridiculous than "Merry Christmas."*) "Because I fell in love." Good afternoon. (*He turns back to his work.*)

FRED. You never came to see me before I married. Why give it as a reason for not coming now?

SCROOGE. Good afternoon.

FRED. I want nothing from you. I ask nothing of you. Why cannot we be friends?

SCROOGE. Good afternoon.

FRED. I am sorry with all my heart to find you so resolute. We have never had any quarrel to which I have been a party. But I have made the visit in homage to Christmas, and I'll keep my Christmas humor to the last. So, a merry Christmas, uncle! (*From his coat, he pulls a small wrapped package and sets it down on* SCROOGE's *desk. Then, he turns for the door.*)

SCROOGE. Good afternoon!

FRED. (*Turning back.*) And a Happy New Year! (*He exits.*)

SCROOGE. Good afternoon! (*Turning on* CRATCHIT.) And you're another fellow. My clerk, with fifteen shillings a week, a wife and family, talking about a merry Christmas. I'll retire to bedlam.

(*A knock on the door, and two* PORTLY GENTLEMEN— *the* FIRST *is* LEMON *and the* SECOND *is* FORSTER— *enter*.)

FIRST PORTLY GENTLEMAN. Scrooge and Marley's, I believe? Have I the pleasure of addressing Mister Scrooge, or Mister Marley?

SCROOGE. Mister Marley has been dead these seven years. He died seven years ago this very night.

SECOND PORTLY GENTLEMAN. (*Handing* SCROOGE *their credentials*.) We have no doubt his liberality is well-represented by his surviving partner. (SCROOGE *examines the credentials and hands them back distastefully*.)

FIRST PORTLY GENTLEMAN. At this festive time of the year, Mister Scrooge, it is more than usually desirable that we should make some slight provision for the poor and destitute, who suffer greatly at the present time. Many thousands are in want of common necessities. Hundreds of thousands are in want of common comforts, sir.

SCROOGE. Are there no prisons?

FIRST PORTLY GENTLEMAN. Plenty of prisons.

SCROOGE. And the workhouses? Are they still in operation?

FIRST PORTLY GENTLEMAN. They are. I wish I could say they were not.

SCROOGE. (*Considering*.) Oh. I was afraid, from what you said at first, that something had occurred to stop them in their useful course. I'm very glad to hear it.

SECOND PORTLY GENTLEMAN. Under the impression that they scarcely furnish cheer of mind or body, a few of us are endeavoring to raise a fund to buy the poor some meat and drink, and means of warmth. We choose this time because it is a time, of all others, when want is keenly felt, and abundance rejoices. What shall I put you down for? (*He opens a small notebook, prepared to record* SCROOGE's *donation.*)

SCROOGE. Nothing.

SECOND PORTLY GENTLEMAN. You wish to be anonymous?

SCROOGE. I wish to be left alone. Since you ask me what I wish, gentlemen, that is my answer. I don't make myself merry at Christmas, and I can't afford to make idle people merry. I help support the establishments I have mentioned— they cost enough, and those who are badly off must go there.

FIRST PORTLY GENTLEMAN. Many can't go there. And many would rather die.

SCROOGE. If they would rather die, they had better do it, and decrease the surplus population. Besides—I don't know that.

FIRST PORTLY GENTLEMAN. But you might know it.

SCROOGE. It's not my business. It's enough for a man to understand his own business, and not interfere with other people's. Mine occupies me constantly.

SECOND PORTLY GENTLEMAN. But, Mister Scrooge—

SCROOGE. (*Showing them to the door.*) Good afternoon.

SECOND PORTLY GENTLEMAN. I can only say, Mister Scrooge, that I hope you will consider the spirit of the day, and think again. Here is my card.

SCROOGE. (*Taking the card, and tearing it slowly.*) Bah. Humbug. (*The two* PORTLY GENTLEMEN *exit.* SCROOGE *feeds the torn card to the fire.* HELEN *and* CHARLEY *enter through the turret door as* CAROLLERS. *They pause, as* SCROOGE *stands at the fireplace, and begin to sing "The Christmas Child."* SCROOGE *turns, and grabs a poker. He walks quickly up the steps of the turret, and the* CHILDREN, *frightened, stop their singing.* CHARLEY *slowly takes off his cap, and holds it out.* SCROOGE *raises the poker over his head.*) Quiet! (*The* CHILDREN *scurry away.* SCROOGE *comes back down the steps.*) Beggars. Pests. (*Off-stage, one of the actors rings a handbell. It is five o'clock.* SCROOGE *checks his watch, and* CRATCHIT *bolts from his desk. He snuffs his candle, and any that are nearby, and puts on a comforter which has been hanging on the coat rack. He approaches* SCROOGE, *who is likewise making ready to leave.*) You'll be wanting all day tomorrow, I suppose?

CRATCHIT. If quite convenient, sir.

SCROOGE. (*Taking some coins from a money bag, and paying him.*) It's not convenient, and it's not fair. If I was to stop your wages half-a-crown, you'd think yourself ill-used, I'll be bound. And yet, you don't think me ill-used when I pay a day's wages for no work.

CRATCHIT. It's only once a year, Mister Scrooge.

SCROOGE. A poor excuse for picking a man's pocket every twenty-fifth of December. But I suppose you must have the whole day. Be here all the earlier next morning.

CRATCHIT. Yes, sir. Thank you, Mister Scrooge. (*He moves to exit, then turns back.*) And a merry Christmas, Mister Scrooge. (*He exits.*)

SCROOGE. "A merry Christmas, Mister Scrooge." Bah. Humbug.

(*Making certain that no one sees, he carefully unwraps the package* FRED *left on his desk. He peeks inside, shuts it up quickly, and locks it in the safe. He stands, and narrates as* DICKENS. *By the time this speech is over, there are no lights on the stage.*)

DICKENS. Scrooge took his melancholy dinner in his usual melancholy tavern; and, having read all the newspapers, and beguiled the rest of the evening with his banker's book, went home to bed. (*The lecturn is cleared from the turret.*) Now, it is a fact that there was nothing at all particular about the knocker on his door, except that it was very large. It is also a fact that Scrooge had seen it, night and morning, during his whole residence in that place; also that Scrooge had as little of what is called fancy about him as any man in the City of London. Let it also be borne in mind that Scrooge had not bestowed one thought on Marley since the last mention of his dead partner that afternoon. (*The last light is extinguished.* SCROOGE *moves Upstage Right toward the door, with a candle in his hand.*) And then, let any man explain, if he can, how it happened that Scrooge, having his key in the lock of the door, saw in the knocker, not a knocker, but— [SOUND EFFECT #1: The low howling of wind, until the candle goes out.]

(*He reverts to* SCROOGE. *A black figure—*FORSTER, *in the black cloak, hood resting on his shoulders—is standing at the door.* SCROOGE *lights the candle, and, as he lifts it, it illuminates* FORSTER'S *face. He has the large handkerchief wrapped around his chin, tied at the crown of his head.*)

SCROOGE. —Marley's face! (*He quickly backs away in shock; the candle goes out.* FORSTER *draws the hood over his face.* SCROOGE *relights the candle and holds it up, seeing nothing.*) Bah. (*He puts his key in the "door."* FORSTER *squeaks, like a large old door swinging open, then disappears behind the real door, slamming it shut.* [SOUND EFFECT #1A: a slamming door, with reverberation.] *A pause.* SCROOGE *relights the candle, and examines the inside of the door—half-expecting to be terrified by the sight of* MARLEY'S *pigtail sticking out into the hall. But there is nothing. He slides two bolts on the door shut.*) Humbug. (*He goes to the window seat, removes his coat, and takes from the storage unit a nightgown, a long cap with a tassle, and a shawl.* [SOUND EFFECT #2: Low sound of wind. It quickly fades.] SCROOGE *crosses to the fireplace.*) Humbug. (*He sits on a stool by the fire, and takes a pan of gruel and a spoon from near the fireplace and eats. Suddenly, the bells on the wall begin to clang;*

first softly, then louder, until they are jangling furiously.
[SOUND EFFECT #3: the bells on the wall are joined by louder, deeper bells, also quite loudly. A loud gong is heard, and the sounds die as quickly as they began.]) Humbug! It's nothing! It's the wind! (*A pause.* SCROOGE *sits rigidly on his stool. Heavy steps are heard upon the stairs.* [SOUND EFFECT #4: chains are being dragged up the stairs.]) It's humbug still! I won't believe it! (*The upper right door swings open* [SOUND EFFECT #4a: A crash of thunder.], *and a bright, eerie light illuminates the doorway.* MARLEY'S GHOST—FORSTER, *in a ragged suit, wrapped in the chains from the horse collar—enters. As he does, the eerie light dies out, and a dim light comes up in the room.*) How now? What do you want with me?

MARLEY. Much.

SCROOGE. Who are you?

MARLEY. Ask me who I was.

SCROOGE. Who *were* you, then?

MARLEY. In life, I was your partner, Jacob Marley.

SCROOGE. Can you sit down?

MARLEY. I can.

SCROOGE. Do it, then.

MARLEY. (*Sits in a chair opposite* SCROOGE.) You don't believe in me.

SCROOGE. I don't.

MARLEY. What evidence would you have of my reality beyond that of your senses?

SCROOGE. I don't know.

MARLEY. Why do you doubt your senses?

SCROOGE. Because a little thing affects them. A slight disorder of the stomach makes them cheats. You may be an undigested bit of beef, a blot of mustard, a crumb of cheese, a fragment of underdone potato. There's more of gravy than of grave about you, whatever you are. Do you see this toothpick? (*Holding one up.*)

MARLEY. I do.

SCROOGE. You are not looking at it.

MARLEY. I see it, notwithstanding.

SCROOGE. I have but to swallow this, and be for the rest of my days persecuted by a legion of goblins, all of my own creation. Humbug, I tell you. Humbug! (MARLEY *raises a frightful cry—a loud, melancholy wail—which sends* SCROOGE *scurrying behind his stool at the fireplace.*) Mercy! Dreadful apparition, why do you trouble me?

MARLEY. Man of worldly mind! Do you believe in me, or not?

SCROOGE. I do, I must. But why do you walk the earth, and why do you come to me?

MARLEY. It is required of every man that the spirit within him should walk abroad among his fellow man, and travel far and wide. If that spirit goes not forth in life, it is condemned to do so after death. It is doomed to wander through the world, and witness what it cannot share but might have shared on earth, and turned to happiness.

SCROOGE. You are wrapped in chains. Tell me why?

MARLEY. I wear the chain I forged in life. I made it, link by link, and yard by yard. I girded it on of my own free will, and of my own free will I wore it. Is its pattern strange to you?

SCROOGE. It is.

MARLEY. Or would you know the weight and length of the strong coil you bear yourself? It was full as heavy and as long as this, seven Christmas Eves ago. You have labored on it since. It is a ponderous chain!

SCROOGE. Old Jacob Marley, tell me more. Speak comfort to me!

MARLEY. I have none to give. A very little more is all that is permitted me. I cannot rest, I cannot stay, I cannot linger anywhere. My spirit never walked beyond our counting-house. In life, my spirit never roved beyond the narrow limits of our money-changing hole. Weary journies lie before me.

SCROOGE. You must have been very slow about it, Jacob.

MARLEY. Slow?

SCROOGE. Seven years dead, and travelling all the time.

MARLEY. The whole time, on the wings of the wind. No rest, no peace, incessant torture of remorse. (*Again he sends up a wail, and rattles his chains.*)

SCROOGE. But you were always a good man of business, Jacob.

MARLEY. Business! Mankind was my business! The common welfare was my business! Charity, mercy, forbearance were all my business. The dealings of my trade were but a drop in the comprehensive ocean of my business!

SCROOGE. Don't be hard on me, Jacob!

MARLEY. My time is nearly gone. How it is that I appear before you in a shape that you can see, I may not tell. I am here tonight to warn you that you have yet a chance of escaping my fate. A chance of my procuring, Ebenezer.

SCROOGE. You were always a good friend to me, Jacob. Thank'ee!

MARLEY. You will be haunted by three spirits.

SCROOGE. Is that the chance you mentioned, Jacob?

MARLEY. It is.

SCROOGE. I think I'd rather not.

MARLEY. Without their visits, you cannot hope to shun the path I tread. (*He crosses to the Downstage window.*) Look you, down upon the people of this planet, your fellow creatures crawling, senses shut, through life. Many of them are known to you. You see them on the streets, in the shops, on the Exchanges. They go about their business, seldom lifting their eyes to the crying children, to the inhuman misery that surrounds them. But what is this misery to what they will know when, gone from this life, they seek to interfere for good in human affairs, and discover that they have lost the power forever? Oh, captive bound and double-ironed, not to know that any human spirit, working kindly in its own sphere, will find its mortal life too short for its

usefulness to mankind! Not to know that no amount of
eternal regret can make amends for a life's opportunities
misused. Yet, such are these. (*To* SCROOGE.) Expect the
first spirit tomorrow, when the bell tolls one.

SCROOGE. Couldn't I take 'em all at once and have it
over, Jacob?

MARLEY. Expect the second on the next night at the same
hour. The third upon the next night when the last stroke of
twelve has ceased to vibrate. Look to see me no more. And,
for your own sake, look that you remember what has passed
between us!

(*He exits through the door, facing* SCROOGE. *Though he is
out of sight, the tail of his chain is visible, and* SCROOGE
follows it, until it winds out of sight. [SOUND
EFFECT #5: THUNDER.] *As soon as the chain is
gone, the door slams shut, and the bolts shoot across.
A pause.* SCROOGE *tries the door. It is locked tight.
The room is silent.*)

SCROOGE. Bah . . . (*He hasn't the heart to squeeze
out a "humbug." He hurries to bed, hops in, and blows
out the light. A peep.*) Humbug. (*A pause. Then, the handbell rings one.*) One! It was past two when I went to bed.
An icicle must have gotten into the works! (*He lights a
candle, sitting up in bed. Suddenly, we hear a strange
tremulo on the violin, then a run up one string. The turret
is lit, and there, violin and bow in hand, is* STANFIELD,
as the GHOST OF CHRISTMAS PAST.) Are you the Spirit, sir,
whose coming was fortold me?

CHRISTMAS PAST. (*Gentle, childlike, and somehow far
away.*) I am.

SCROOGE. Who and what are you?

CHRISTMAS PAST. I am the Ghost of Christmas Past.

SCROOGE. Long past?

CHRISTMAS PAST. No, your past.

SCROOGE. What business brings you?

CHRISTMAS PAST. Your welfare.

SCROOGE. I'm much obliged, but I can't help thinking that a night of unbroken rest would be more conducive to that end.

CHRISTMAS PAST. Your reclamation, then.

SCROOGE. Bah. What reclamation is there in the past. I don't want to see it.

CHRISTMAS PAST. Why not?

SCROOGE. Because it is unpleasant to me. No good can come of it.

CHRISTMAS PAST. Take heed! Remember what you have seen already! (*This has its effect on* SCROOGE.) Rise, and walk with me!

SCROOGE. (*Getting out of bed, and approaching the* GHOST.) I? But I am mortal, and likely to fall.

CHRISTMAS PAST. Bear but a touch of my hand, and you shall be upheld in more than this! (*He extends the end of his bow, which* SCROOGE *grabs onto, and whisks him up to the turret. With a wave of the bow*.) Is this place familiar to you?

(CHARLEY *enters as* YOUNG EBENEZER, *with a book in his hand. He takes the stool to the middle of the second level, and sits. He opens the book and reads.*)

SCROOGE. Good heavens! I was at school in this place! I was a boy here!

CHRISTMAS PAST. These are but shadows of the things that have been. They have no consciousness of us. (CHARLEY *lifts his eyes from the book, and sighs*.) The school is not quite deserted. A solitary child, neglected by his friends, is left there still. (YOUNG EBENEZER *begins to hum "The Christmas Child."*)

SCROOGE. (*Recognizing him, goes to him, and places a hand on his shoulder*.) Poor boy.

(HELEN *enters as* FAN, YOUNG EBENEZER'S *sister. She doesn't see* SCROOGE; *she runs to* YOUNG EBENEZER. *He is ecstatic to see her.*)

FAN. Ebenezer! Dear, dear brother! I have come to take you home!

SCROOGE. Fan!

YOUNG EBENEZER. Home, Fan?

FAN. Yes, home, for good and all. Father is so much kinder than he used to be. He spoke so gently to me one night that I wasn't afraid to ask him once more if you might come home. And he said yes, you should. He sent me in a coach to bring you.

YOUNG EBENEZER. This *is* a merry Christmas, Fan!

FAN. We're to be together all Christmas, and have the merriest time in the world. Let's get your trunk! (*They exit.*)

CHRISTMAS PAST. Always a delicate creature, whom a breath might have withered.

SCROOGE. (*Looking after them.*) But she had a large heart.

CHRISTMAS PAST. So she had. She died a woman, and had, as I think, children.

SCROOGE. One child.

CHRISTMAS PAST. True. Your nephew.

SCROOGE. I wish . . .

CHRISTMAS PAST. What is the matter?

SCROOGE. Nothing, nothing. There were some children singing a Christmas carol at my door last night. I should like to have given them something, that's all. (*The lights go full.*)

CHRISTMAS PAST. Do you know this place?

SCROOGE. (*Something about this new place jogs his memory.*) Know it? I was apprenticed here!

(LEMON, *as* FEZZIWIG, *a warehouse owner to whom*

SCROOGE *was apprenticed long ago, bustles in, wearing the Welsh wig.*)

FEZZIWIG. Yo ho, there! Ebenezer! Dick!
SCROOGE. Why, it's old Fezziwig! Bless his heart, it's Fezziwig, alive again!

(FREDERICK *enters as* YOUNG SCROOGE, *now about twenty-one, as cheerful as old* SCROOGE *is dour. With him is* FORSTER, *as* DICK WILKINS, *also an apprentice, and also about twenty-one.*)

FEZZIWIG. (*Moving a chair upstage.*) No more work tonight. Christmas Eve, Dick! Christmas, Ebenezer! Let's have the place cleared away before a man can say "Jack Robinson"!

(DICK *and* EBENEZER *set to work, clearing away tables and chairs. They clear away a space large enough to permit dancing, singing as they go.*)

SCROOGE. Dick Wilkins, to be sure! Bless me, yes. He was very much attached to me was Dick. Poor Dick. Dear, dear . . .
FEZZIWIG. Hilli-ho! Clear away, my lads, and let's have lot's of room here! Hilli-ho, Dick! Chirrip, Ebenezer!

(*As they work, in comes* MRS. STANFIELD *as* BELLE, SCROOGE's *fiancée, and the* FEZZIWIGS' *daughter;* CATHERINE *as* MRS. FEZZIWIG; *and* HELEN *and* CHARLEY *as little* FEZZIWIGS. *The children should also have little Welsh wigs. More singing; punch is poured, and partaken of.*)

FEZZIWIG. (*Quieting the crowd.*) My dears, it's Christmas Eve. A toast to that glorious occasion! May tomorrow, and the whole of the new year find us merry, content, and above all, filled with the happy good will of the season toward all our fellows!

EVERYONE. Bravo! To Christmas! (*Etc.*)

FEZZIWIG. And, in honor of the great day, I have engaged the services of the most renowned musician in the City of London. His nimble tricks over and amongst the strings of that most splendid of instruments are too well-known that I should relate them. You all know him; you're all no doubt acquainted with his miraculous capacity to raise the spirits of even the most mortuary of countenances. Ladies and gentlemen, I give you the highly valued . . . (*With a flourish, he indicates* CHRISTMAS PAST, *who stands ready with violin and bow.*)

CHRISTMAS PAST. (*As the crowd applauds.*) My, my. Don't deserve it, really. Ladies and gents: "The Christmas Child."

(*He—or, magically, the violin alone—strikes up a reel, based on "The Christmas Child." The dancing begins.* SCROOGE *acts like a man possessed, laughing, dancing among the partners, jesting if someone misses a step, etc. The dancing ends amid loud applause for the fiddler, which* CHRISTMAS PAST *acknowledges with a deep bow.*)

CHRISTMAS PAST. (*As the guests gather around the trunk, for the opening of some gifts for the children.*) A small matter, to make these silly folk so full of gratitude.

SCROOGE. Small?

CHRISTMAS PAST. Why, is it not? He has spent but a few pounds of your mortal money—three or four, perhaps. Is that so much that he deserves praise?

SCROOGE. It isn't that at all, Spirit. He had the power to render us happy or unhappy; to make our service light or burdensome. The happiness he gave was quite as great as if it had cost a fortune . . . (*He is suddenly quiet.*)

CHRISTMAS PAST. What is the matter?

SCROOGE. Nothing particular.

CHRISTMAS PAST. Something, I think.

SCROOGE. No, no. I should like to be able to say a word or two to my clerk just now. That's all.

(*A cheer from the crowd, as a toy drum is unwrapped, and* CHARLEY *tries it out.*)

FEZZIWIG. My dears, the hour grows late. Before we depart, however, Mrs. Fezziwig and I have an announcement. An announcement of a most auspicious nature.

SCROOGE. Spirit, show me no more.

FEZZIWIG. As you know, Mrs. Fezziwig and I have labored these many years to rear a very particular child. The fruits of our labor, I am happy to say, are most satisfactory—more than satisfactory. They are summed up in one beautiful word—Belle. (*Applause.*) Now at the very dawn, the very ripeness of her youth and beauty, she has surrendered to the wiles of one of you in this very room. One to whom I've furnished shelter, food, and a warm bed.

DICK WILKINS. A sore back and aching eyes, too!

FEZZIWIG. Yes, I'll not deny he's the hardest-working apprentice ever to balance a book or close an account. Come Spring, our lovely Belle shall wed that most industrious of young men, Mister Ebenezer Scrooge! (*Applause.*)

DICK WILKINS. A dance! A dance from the couple!

(*The lights are dimmed, and* YOUNG SCROOGE *and* BELLE *embrace, and dance a slow waltz based on "The Christmas Child."*)

SCROOGE. (*Scarcely able to watch.*) Spirit, take me home.

(*As the short dance ends,* YOUNG SCROOGE *and* BELLE *drift apart,* YOUNG SCROOGE *to the desk, which was moved Downstage. He sits, and becomes absorbed in his work.* BELLE *approaches him. Some time has passed since the dance.)*

BELLE. It matters little to you; very little. Another idol has displaced me. If it can cheer and comfort you in times to come, as I would have tried to do, I have no just cause to grieve.

YOUNG SCROOGE. (*Annoyed at this distraction.*) What idol has displaced you?

BELLE. A golden one.

YOUNG SCROOGE. This is the even-handed dealing of the world. There is nothing on which it is so hard as poverty; and there is nothing it professes to condemn so severely as the pursuit of wealth.

BELLE. You fear the world too much. All your other hopes have merged into the hope of being beyond the world's reproach. I have seen your nobler aspirations fall off, one by one, until one passion, Gain, engrosses you. Have I not?

YOUNG SCROOGE. (*Checking his watch.*) What then? Even if I have grown so much wiser, what then? I am not changed toward you. (*A pause.*) Am I?

BELLE. Our contract is an old one. It was made when we were both poor and content to be so, until in good time, we could improve our fortunes. You are changed. When it was made, you were another man.

YOUNG SCROOGE. I was a boy.

BELLE. Your own feeling tells you that you are not what you were. I am. How often I have thought of this does not matter. It is enough that I *have* thought of it, and can release you.

YOUNG SCROOGE. Have I ever sought release?

BELLE. In words, no. Never.

YOUNG SCROOGE. In what, then?

BELLE. In a changed nature, an altered spirit. In everything that made my love of any worth or value in your sight.

If we had never had our past, would you seek me out and try to win me now?

YOUNG SCROOGE. You think not.

BELLE. I would think otherwise if I could. But if you were free today, could I believe you would choose a girl with so small a dowery? You, who now weigh everything by gain? Or, if you did choose her, do I not know that your regret would surely follow? I do. And I release you. (*She takes a ring from her finger, and presses it into* YOUNG SCROOGE's *hand.*) With a full heart, for the love of him you once were. May you be happy in the life you have chosen. (*She exits. A pause.* YOUNG SCROOGE *stands, but does not move.*)

SCROOGE. (*Pleading.*) Go to her, you fool! (*As* YOUNG SCROOGE *stands there.*) You fool! (YOUNG SCROOGE *wraps the ring in a piece of paper, and shuts it up in a drawer in the desk.*) Spirit, show me no more. Why do you delight to torture me?

CHRISTMAS PAST. I told you these were shadows of things that have been. That they are what they are, do not blame me.

SCROOGE. Leave me, take me back! Haunt me no longer.

CHRISTMAS PAST. As you wish. (*With a wave of his hand, he vanishes, and* SCROOGE *is left alone in the darkness.*) Belle . . . Belle . . . (THE CHILD *appears on the turret.*)

THE CHILD. Where's the boy?

DICKENS. I haven't forgotten. He's coming.

THE CHILD. Good.

DICKENS. What do you think?

THE CHILD. It's alright. The song's nice. (*He sings.*)
"Oh, Christmas Child,
Oh, Christmas Child,
Why do you cry little Christmas Child?
Old men need your smile."

(*The lights fade out.*)

ACT TWO

As the lights come up, FORSTER *is standing on the turret.
On his head is a flowing white wig; a matching beard
and moustache are on his face. At the Downstage end
of the second level is the coat rack, on which is hung
a long, green mantle. A quilt, neatly folded, is on
the window seat.*

FORSTER. (*Experimenting with a character.*) "Enter,
Ebenezer Scrooge!" No. "Enter! Ebeenezer Scrooge!" (*A
pause.*) Hmmm. It's missing something. What? (*He goes
to the trunk and pulls out* FREDERICK's *top hat. He then
crosses to the coat rack, and puts the beard, wig, and
hat on top of the mantle. He stands back for a look.*) No.
(*He puts the hat back in the trunk, and tries* CHARLEY's
cap instead.) Too juvenile. (*He goes to the desk, where*
DICKENS' *wig lays. He tries this instead of the other wig.*
LEMON *enters, a glass of punch in his hand. He stands
watching.*) Heavens, no. (*He takes the wig off the coat
rack and puts it back on the desk.*) Well? Don't just stand
there like a stick of wood. Inspire me.

LEMON. I spotted you sneaking away. (*He comes down
the steps, and goes to the fireplace, where he stokes the
fire.*) What are you up to? Not giving up literary criticism
for a haberdashery, I hope?

FORSTER. This, my dear Lemon, is the next ghost: the
Ghost of Christmas . . . something-or-other.

LEMON. Really? To be played by you, I presume?

FORSTER. Naturally.

LEMON. (*Sitting on the stool near the fireplace.*) Do you
think the others will co-operate? Such advance planning
may not be strictly fair.

FORSTER. Of course they'll co-operate. It benefits the
story immensely. (*A pause.*) But it's missing something.

LEMON. It does look something less than . . . ghostly.

FORSTER. What are they up to downstairs?

LEMON. He has them on another scavenger hunt. (*Watching* FORSTER *search through the trunk.*) Anything proper in the trunk?

FORSTER. Some chalk, in case Stanfield is seized with the urge to draw scenery. (*Standing.*) Here, let's see what it looks like. (*He gets the quilt, giving* LEMON *one side of it. They unfold it.*)

LEMON. Where did you find this?

FORSTER. In the linen closet.

LEMON. (*Chuckling.*) Pardon me, Forster, but the thought of you, who strikes unholy terror into the hearts of fledgling writers, plundering a linen closet so that you may run about as a ghost—well, it's droll. I think I'll put it in the next edition of *Punch*.

FORSTER. Don't you dare. (*They are holding the quilt before the coat rack.*) Now, bring it down slowly. (*They do.*) Well? What do you think?

LEMON. I think it looks like a scarecrow.

FORSTER. You're right. It needs something to top it off, to round it out. (*A pause, as he and* LEMON *exchange glances. He takes the beard and cloak off the rack.*) Come with me. (*He pulls* LEMON *to the window seat.*) Get up here.

LEMON. What?

FORSTER. Get up here. Come, come. (*He helps* LEMON *up.*)

LEMON. What the devil . . .

FORSTER. (*He gives* LEMON *the mantle and beard.*) Now put these on. Good.

LEMON. (*Putting them on.*) My idea of Christmas Eve is good company, a decent meal, and a warm parlour.

FORSTER. (*Enveloping himself in the mantle.*) Get on my shoulders.

LEMON. What!?

FORSTER. Sit on my shoulders.

LEMON. I don't like heights. And acrobatics is not at all—

FORSTER. (*As* LEMON *climbs gingerly onto his shoulders.*) Look at it this way. If I should collapse, we'll both be in the parlour. (*With a grunt, he tries to lift him.*) My God. Are you sure you haven't eaten?

LEMON. Well? Are you going to lift me or not?

FORSTER. I'm trying. One . . . two . . . three. (*He tries to lift* LEMON. *He fails.*)

DICKENS. (*Off.*) Are we ready?

LEMON. Are *we* ready? (*A pause.*)

FORSTER. I'm afraid, Lemon, this is not going to work.

LEMON. (*Getting off* FORSTER's *shoulders.*) Of course not. It took you long enough to see the blinding light of that revelation.

FORSTER. (*Stretching his back.*) I assure you, Lemon, it had nothing whatsoever to do with light. Help me hide these things.

LEMON. Here. In the window seat. (*They stow the beard, wig, and mantle in the window seat.*) Ghosts are not my forte. I specialize in more substantial beings.

FORSTER. I still need something . . .

LEMON. (*Spotting a large wreath hanging above the fireplace, and taking it from the wall.*) Here, try this. (*He puts it on* FORSTER's *head.*) That should sit more lightly on your troubled brow. It'll give him a start, too. The coat rack.

FORSTER. Oh, yes. (*He grabs the coat rack, and puts it back on the turret, where it was at the end of Act One.* DICKENS *bounds up the stairs and enters.*)

DICKENS. Gentlemen! (*Tweaking the wreath on* FORSTER's *head.*) I see you're prepared to carry on the tale.

FORSTER. (*Quickly taking it off, hiding it behind his back.*) We are. That is, we . . .

DICKENS. Excellent. (*Looking around.*) The room is in

order. Good. (*He turns to go, then turns back.*) I'm arranging a small processional. (*He exits.*)

LEMON. Evidently, we're in for a start, as well.

DICKENS. (*Issuing instructions from downstairs.*) Don't drop those, Frederick. No, *you're* in front, and *you're* behind. Up you go, Charley. You're first.

FORSTER. Well, I'm glad nothing out of the ordinary is happening this Christmas.

DICKENS. (*Off.*) Don't eat them, Stanny. Carry them. (*A pause. LEMON and FORSTER exchange a glance, then turn their eyes toward the door. The silence ends as a procession, lead by CHARLEY, winds into the room. CHARLEY carries a small goose on a platter. He's followed by HELEN, carrying a pudding; STANFIELD with a large bowl of apples and oranges; CATHERINE with a tray of old mugs; MRS. STANFIELD with a box of tinware which has seen better days; FREDERICK, who is juggling apples and oranges; and DICKENS.*) Don't bruise that fruit, Frederick.

FREDERICK. An impossibility! Newton defied!

LEMON. Are we about to cannibalize our dinner? For the sake of the story?

DICKENS. Never fear, Uncle Porpoise. This is only the beginning of the feast.

LEMON. I certainly hope so. (*Regarding the goose held by CHARLEY, who is standing nearby.*) The poor beast is stunted.

CHARLEY. It's not so small if you ask me.

DICKENS. No, it's not the main course. In her wisdom, Mrs. Dickens concluded that a smaller goose ought to be procured in the event that the first goose prove not to be large enough. You'll be happy to know, Uncle Porpoise, that the senior goose is safe and simmering in the oven.

CATHERINE. Not that he didn't try to get that one, too.

MRS. STANFIELD. There's barely a thing left downstairs. Mary is positively in a turmoil.

CATHERINE. And she should be, having dinner stolen from under her nose like that.

DICKENS. Nonsense. Mary's an excellent woman, and a cook most adaptable to any situation. In any event, I've sent her home, where she ought to be on Christmas Eve.

STANFIELD. I say, Dickens, may we—for the sake of the children, that is—put these things down?

DICKENS. Yes, of course. Edibles on the window seat, utensils on the desk.

FORSTER. (*Looking at the mugs on the tray as the women move past him.*) My God, have you been to a pawnshop?

DICKENS. No, my dear Forster. They are from the cellar: relics of my ancient past. Frederick will recognize them as the family tinware—which did, in fact, spend some days in the local pawnshop. We have yet to examine some of the families we have introduced. These few domestic items, along with what we already have, will help us to furnish their lodgings. (*Putting on the wig, night gown, and sleeping cap.*) I've seen another vision.

LEMON. Lord help us.

DICKENS. This time, the child was singing. So warm up your voices.

FORSTER. (*To* LEMON.) It could be worse. What if he were flying?

DICKENS. We left Ebenezer Scrooge in bed, vainly trying to recall and mend his unpleasant past, and wondering what variety of spirits await him in the present and future. (*He puts on the nose and glasses.*) Gentlemen of the free-and-easy sort, who pride themselves on being acquainted with a move or two . . . (*He turns down the gas lamp and gets into bed. Meanwhile,* FORSTER *disappears behind the quilt, which is held up by* LEMON *and* STANFIELD, *just in front of the window seat.*) express the wide range of their capacity for adventure by observing that they are good for anything from pitch-and-toss to manslaughter. Without venturing for Scrooge quite as heartily as this, I don't mind calling on you to believe that he was ready for a good broad field of strange appearances, and that nothing between a baby and a rhinocerous would have astonished him very much. (*A pause.*)

Now, being prepared for almost anything, he was by no means prepared for nothing. (*A pause.*) The bell tolled one. (*It tolls from behind the quilt.*) And no shape appeared. Five minutes. (*Pause.*) Ten minutes. (*Pause.*) A quarter of an hour went by. (*Pause.*) Yet nothing came.

(*The light in the fireplace begins to glow brightly.* [SOUND EFFECT #6: *Deep echoing laughter, growing louder and louder. When it dies out, a booming voice is heard from behind the quilt.*])

VOICE. Enter, Ebenezer Scrooge! (SCROOGE *gets out of bed, as the quilt drops away, revealing* FORSTER *in the wig, beard, and mantle, as the* GHOST OF CHRISTMAS PRESENT. *His head is crowned by the wreath* LEMON *pulled off the wall. He is standing on the window seat, seemingly much at home, reclining against the rafters.*) Come in and know me better, man! (SCROOGE *approaches meekly.*) I am the Ghost of Christmas Present. Look upon me. You have never seen the like of me before!

SCROOGE. Never.

CHRISTMAS PRESENT. You have never walked forth with the younger members of my family, my brothers born in these later years?

SCROOGE. I'm afraid I have not. Have you many brothers, Spirit?

CHRISTMAS PRESENT. More than eighteen hundred.

SCROOGE. A tremendous family to provide for.

CHRISTMAS PRESENT. Nor have I ever seen the likes of *you*. You're so sour, the blood's gone bad in your veins.

SCROOGE. Spirit, conduct me where you will. I went forth last night on compulsion, and I learned a lesson which is working still. Tonight, if you have ought to teach me, let me profit by it.

CHRISTMAS PRESENT. Profit? Touch my robe!

(SCROOGE *does so.* [SOUND EFFECT #7: Six chimes of a mantle clock.] *As the chimes sound,* CATHERINE, HELEN, *and* FREDERICK *enter as* MRS. CRATCHIT, PETER CRATCHIT, *and* BELINDA CRATCHIT. PETER *carries the desk—or another similar table which may be substituted for the desk in all of Act Two—Down Center on the second level.* MRS. CRATCHIT *covers it with a table cloth, and* BELINDA *sets two candlesticks on it.*)

MRS. CRATCHIT. Whatever has gotten your precious father, then? And your brother, Tiny Tim? And Martha wasn't as late last Christmas by half-an-hour. (MRS. STAN-FIELD *enters as* MARTHA.)

MARTHA. Here's Martha, mother!

BELINDA. Here's Martha! There's such a goose, Martha!

MRS. CRATCHIT. Why bless you my dear, how late you are. They're keeping you longer and longer at the milliner's. (BELINDA *goes to the door to keep watch for* CRATCHIT *and* TINY TIM.)

MARTHA. We had a tremendous deal of work to finish up last night, and had to clear away this morning.

MRS. CRATCHIT. Working on Christmas Eve! Well, never mind so long as you're here. Sit down by the fire, my dear, and have a warm.

BELINDA. Here's father coming! Hide, Martha, hide!

MARTHA. (*Who's not had the chance to sit down, yet.*) Where?

(*Quickly, they settle on beneath the table. No sooner is she hidden then* STANFIELD *enters as* CRATCHIT, *with* CHARLEY, *as* TINY TIM, *on his shoulder.* TIM *is carrying the crutch.*)

CRATCHIT. Merry Christmas, my dears! (*Putting* TIM *into*

PETER's *arms in order that he may take off his comforter, which he hangs on the coat rack.*) Merry Christmas, Peter.

PETER. Merry Christmas, father!

CRATCHIT. (*Noticing* MARTHA's *absence.*) Why, where's our Martha?

MRS. CRATCHIT. Not coming.

CRATCHIT. Not coming? Not coming upon Christmas Day?

MRS. CRATCHIT. She had so much work at the milliner's. They sent someone 'round to tell the families that all the girls would be staying.

CRATCHIT. (*Very much let down.*) Oh. Well, if she feels she must stay, we'll abide by her good judgement. But it hardly seems fair . . . to work on Christmas Day.

(*A giggle is heard underneath the table.* CRATCHIT *goes to the table, lifts the table cloth, and* MARTHA *embraces him.*)

MARTHA. I'm here, father. I can't stand to see you disappointed, even for a joke!

CRATCHIT. Well then, we're all together, after all! Then it *will* be a merry Christmas.

MRS. CRATCHIT. Peter, take Tim off to the wash-house. The goose will be ready before we know it.

PETER. (*Who still has* TIM *on his shoulder.*) Right, ma'am. Alright, Timothy. This way. (*They exit through the Up Right door.*)

MRS. CRATCHIT. And tend to the pudding, Belinda. It mustn't be overdone.

BELINDA. (*Sensing the gravity of this possibility.*) What if it were? (*She and* MARTHA *exit, Up Right, determined to save the pudding.*)

MRS. CRATCHIT. (*To* BOB. *They cross to the fireplace and sit.* MRS. CRATCHIT *takes the bowl of fruit, and peels some apples.*) And how did Tim behave at church?

CRATCHIT. As good as gold—and better. Somehow, he gets thoughtful, sitting by himself so much, and he thinks the strangest things you ever heard. He told me, coming home, that he hoped the people saw him in church, because he was a cripple, and it might be pleasant for them to remember upon Christmas Day who made lame beggars walk and blind men see. (*A pause.*) Then, I trotted us 'round to the shop windows, where he gazed for the longest time at the toys. Sensing his spirits beginning to droop, I galloped straight away to Cornhill Street, where, in honor of its being Christmas, we went down the slide twenty times. (TINY TIM *enters, followed by* MARTHA.)

TINY TIM. Twenty-five!

CRATCHIT. (*Taking* TIM *on his lap.*) Right you are, Tim. Twenty-five! (*A pause.*) And all along the way, any number of acquaintances stopped us to remark that Tim is looking stronger and heartier everday . . . (*Another pause.*)

MARTHA. You haven't made the punch yet, father. It can't be Christmas without your special punch.

CRATCHIT. (*Brightening.*) That's a fact. What could I be thinking to forget that? (*Taking a decanter from the mantle, he crosses to the table, where* MARTHA *has just placed the mugs and pitcher.*) Here's Christmas dinner practically on the table, and not a drop of punch in evidence. Easily remedied! (*He adds some of the decanter's contents into the pitcher and stirs.*)

PETER. (*Entering with* BELINDA.) Here we are, perfectly cleaned, and wonderfully starved.

MRS. CRATCHIT. Good. The goose is all but calling to be let out of the oven. Martha, help your father with the punch. (*She exits,* BELINDA *follows her to the door to stand guard.*)

CRATCHIT. No need, no need. All done, and in a trice. (MARTHA *helps him distribute mugs around the table.*)

PETER. Remarkable time, father.

CRATCHIT. Let no man say that old Bob Cratchit can't mix his Christmas punch with the swiftest of 'em.

BELINDA. Here's the goose!

(She exits. MRS. CRATCHIT enters proudly bearing the roast goose on its tray. BELINDA enters again, carrying the pudding. Oohs and aahhs from the family; universal admiration for both bird and pudding.)

PETER. Bravo! A glorious bird! *(They gather around the table.)*

CRATCHIT. Never has there been such a bird! A truly sumptuous-looking fowl, Mrs. Cratchit.

SCROOGE. *(To* CHRISTMAS PRESENT.*)* So small a goose for so large a family.

CRATCHIT. And a pudding! Have you ever seen such a one? I ask you, Martha.

MARTHA. Never. The girls at the shop would be positively ashamed to display theirs anywhere in the vicinity.

BELINDA. Hear, hear!

TINY TIM. They'd not be seen.

CRATCHIT. And you, Master Peter? Have you ever set eyes upon the mortal pudding which could equal this wonder?

PETER. In all my years as a Christmas pudding observer, I've never seen a finer.

CRATCHIT. And that's a high compliment indeed. Tell me a higher one, and I'll use it. Mrs. Cratchit, as for myself, I think that it is your greatest success since our marriage.

MRS. CRATCHIT. Well, it's a great weight off my mind. I don't mind confessing I had my doubts about the quantity of flour.

MARTHA. Never fear, mother. It's perfect.

CRATCHIT. *(Tapping his mug with a spoon.)* Now, before plunging into this splendid feast, I'd like to propose a health. *(He raises his mug, the others do the same.)* A merry Christmas to us all, my dears. God bless us.

FAMILY. God bless us!

TINY TIM. God bless us, every one.

SCROOGE. *(With an interest he's never felt before.)* Spirit, tell me if Tiny Tim will live.

CHRISTMAS PRESENT. I see a vacant seat in the poor chimney corner, and a crutch without an owner, carefully preserved. If these shadows remained unaltered by the future, the child will die.

SCROOGE. Kind Spirit, say he will be spared.

CHRISTMAS PRESENT. If these shadows remain unaltered by the future, none other of my race will find him here. (*Turning on* SCROOGE.) What of it? If he be like to die, he had better do it, and decrease the surplus population. (SCROOGE *turns away, stung by his own words.*) Man, if man you be, forbear that wicked cant until you have discovered what the surplus is, and where it is. Will you decide what men shall live and what men shall die? It might be that, in the sight of Heaven, you are less fit to live than millions like this poor man's child.

SCROOGE. It may be, Spirit. It may be.

CRATCHIT. A toast! A toast, everyone. Mister Scrooge! I give you Mister Scrooge, the founder of the feast. (*A pall descends upon the proceedings, and the family, as one, puts their mugs down.*)

MRS. CRATCHIT. The Founder of the Feast indeed! I wish I had him here. I'd give him a piece of my mind to feast upon, and I hope he'd have good appetite for it.

CRATCHIT. My dear, the children. Christmas Day.

MRS. CRATCHIT. It should be Christmas Day I'm sure, on which we drink the health of such an odious, stingy, hard, unfeeling man as Mister Scrooge. You know he is, Robert. Nobody knows it better than you do.

CRATCHIT. My dear, Christmas Day. (*A pause.*)

MRS. CRATCHIT. I'll drink his health for your sake and the day's. Not for his. A merry Christmas and a happy New Year to him. He'll be very merry and very happy, I have no doubt. (*Raising her mug.*) Mister Scrooge.

THE FAMILY. (*With no enthusiasm whatsoever.*) Mister Scrooge. (*They drink. A pause.*)

TINY TIM. I wouldn't give tuppence for Mister Scrooge.

BELINDA. Either would I.

CRATCHIT. Have an open heart, I beg you. It's Christmas, after all. And I think that, in many ways, Mister Scrooge is a great deal less fortunate than we are.

PETER. Impossible.

CRATCHIT. Not at all. Compare our condition with that of Mister Scrooge. He has no family to gather 'round him, no warmth, no cheer. He has none but his own voice to listen to, and none to answer. I believe he is a great deal less fortunate than we.

CHRISTMAS PRESENT. A clerk who makes fifteen shillings a week, and he counts himself more fortunate than you?

CRATCHIT. Remembering those who are less fortunate, let us say grace. (*The family takes hands.*) Kind father, bless this humble portion. Bless our home, bless our family, bless our happiness. May we share them all with any who should ask, in your name. Amen.

(*The lights dim, and the family vanishes.* [SOUND EFFECT #8: celeste, mantle clock, wind.] SCROOGE *moves toward the family as the lights go out. The dialogue continues over the sound effect.*)

CHRISTMAS PRESENT. You cannot move within that circle.

SCROOGE. Why not, Spirit?

CHRISTMAS PRESENT. Did you not hear the clerk take the measure of his employer? You are drifting alone, outside, and cannot get in. You have no circle.

SCROOGE. There was a time, Spirit, when I had.

CHRISTMAS PRESENT. How many years ago? That kind circle has long since withered, and you have cast it from your heart.

SCROOGE. I deny it, Spirit, I deny it! If any kindness has withered in me, it has done so of its own accord. I had nothing to do with it. If kindness wishes to wither, it withers.

CHRISTMAS PRESENT. Have you not seen, nor heard? You unrepentant little man. You have a long journey to make, and but a short time in which to make it. Let us see another house in this teeming city.

(*With a wave of his hand, the lights come up, and we are in* FRED's *parlour. Also here are* CATHERINE *as* MRS. FRED, MRS. STANFIELD *as* MRS. FRED'S SISTER, *and* STANFIELD *as* TOPPER. *They have brought the punch bowl center of the first level, and have placed it on the high stool.* FRED *has just given them each a long carrot, and they are seated around him, ready for some sort of game.*)

FRED. Everyone have theirs? Good. Now, place it on the end of your nose, like this. (*He places the fat end of the carrot on the tip of his nose. The others do the same.*) Ready? Now repeat after me: (*He assumes a* SCROOGE-*like voice.*) ". . . should be boiled in his own pudding . . ."

THE OTHERS. (*Also intoning as they think* SCROOGE *might.*) ". . . should be boiled in his own pudding . . ."

FRED. ". . . and be buried with a stake of holly through his heart. He should!"

THE OTHERS. ". . . and be buried with a stake of holly through his heart. He should!"

(*They laugh, as* FRED *collects the carrots from them, and places them on the tray next to the punch bowl.*)

FRED. And as I live, he said that Christmas was a humbug! He believed it, too.

MRS. FRED. More shame for him, Fred.

FRED. He's a comical old fellow, that's the truth—though not as pleasant as he might be. However, his offenses carry their own punishment, and I'll have nothing to say against him.

MRS. FRED. I'm sure he's very rich. At least you always tell me so.

FRED. What of that, my dear? His wealth is of no use to him. He doesn't do any good with it. He doesn't make himself comfortable with it. And he hasn't the satisfaction of thinking he is ever going to benefit *us* with it. (*They laugh at the thought of this unlikely occurrence.*)

MRS. FRED. I have no patience with him.

FRED. Oh, I have. I'm sorry for him. I couldn't be angry with him if I tried. Who suffers by his ill whims? Himself, always. Here he takes it into his head to dislike us and he won't come to dine with us. What's the consequence? (*Tossing it off.*) He doesn't lose much of a dinner.

MRS. FRED. Indeed, I think he loses a very good dinner!

MRS. FRED'S SISTER. He does.

FRED. Well, I'm glad to hear it, because I haven't any faith in these young housekeepers. What do you say, Topper?

TOPPER. (*A young chap who very much has his eye on* MRS. FRED'S SISTER—*and everyone knows it.*) I am a bachelor, and a bachelor is a wretched outcast who has no right to express an opinion on the subject. (*And he promptly squeezes* MRS. FRED'S SISTER, *who responds with a giggle.*)

MRS. FRED. Do go on, Fred. (*To the others.*) He never finishes what he begins to say. He's such a ridiculous fellow!

FRED. I was only going to say that the consequence of his disliking us is that he loses some pleasant moments which could do him no harm. I mean to give him the same chance every year—whether he likes it or not. He may rail at Christmas 'til he dies, but he can't help thinking better of it if he finds me going there, in good humor, year after year, and saying, "Uncle Scrooge, how are you?" If it only puts him in a mind to leave his poor clerk fifty pounds, *that's* something. And I think I shook him yesterday.

TOPPER. From the sound of him, I don't see where there's

any more chance of shaking Mister Scrooge than there is of shaking the Rock of Gibralter.

MRS. FRED. Less, I should think.

TOPPER. (*Taking his violin from its case, which has been sitting near the foot of the turret.*) I seem to recall, my dear Fred, that you promised a song would issue from the lovely throat of our hostess. Am I correct sir, or am I mistaken?

FRED. Not mistaken at all. (*To* MRS. FRED.) On your behalf, my dear, I pledged that you would sing us a song befitting the season.

MRS. FRED. You did?

FRED. I had to. It was the only course of preventing Topper from playing his violin. (TOPPER *plays a sour note.*) And as I made the pledge over the punch bowl, you really must oblige. Any promise made near a punch bowl is a binding one, and it's a grave risk to one's honor not to carry through.

TOPPER. If you don't sing, we'll have no recourse but to put this little warbler into the field— (*He squeezes* MRS. FRED'S SISTER *again, and again she giggles.*) and we might all have cause to regret that.

MRS. FRED'S SISTER. I'm a very fine singer. I sing solos in church.

TOPPER. In church? Would you consider a duet?

(MRS. FRED'S SISTER *giggles loudly at this outrageous suggestion, and is rescued by* MRS. FRED, *who hurries her away to the top of the turret.*)

MRS. FRED. Well, we'll both sing—to rescue Fred's honor. I know. The one Fred was taught by his mother.

FRED. Oh, "The Christmas Child." Good, my favorite. Do you know that one, Topper?

TOPPER. I know them all.

(*He plays a brief introduction, and the women sing "The*

Christmas Child.'' As they sing, SCROOGE *recognizes the tune as one he sung as a young boy, and slowly, softly, begins singing with them, in a voice long out of use. Near the end, he realises he is being observed by the* GHOST, *and, more self-consciously than angrily, he stops.)*

THE WOMEN. (*Sing.*)
Oh, Christmas Child,
Oh, Christmas Child,
Why do you cry, little Christmas Child?
Old men need your smile.

''What a world of joy,''
cries the Christmas boy,
''is lost, is lost
in the hearts of men.''

Come you see this sight
on this Christmas night,
A star, a star
is ablaze within.

Oh, Christmas Child,
Oh, Christmas Child,
I see the star, little Christmas Child,
Shining from your heart.

And an old man's heart
shattered wide apart,
With hope, with love
on this Christmas night.
It's the star of cheer
singing ''Peace is here.''
Rejoice, rejoice,
For this wondrous sight.

Oh, Christmas Child,
Oh, Christmas Child,
You've made me wise, little Christmas Child.
I'm your Christmas Child.
(Copyright 1978 Tom Fulton and Michael Griffith. Used by permission.)

(FRED *and* TOPPER *applaud with approval.*)

TOPPER. I commend your choice of songbirds, my dear Fred. What sort of net did you use to catch her?

MRS. FRED. Topper, whatever makes you think *he* caught *me?*

CHRISTMAS PRESENT. A game is in order, I think.

MRS. FRED'S SISTER. A game! Blind man!

TOPPER. (*Taking it up immediately.*) Blind man's buff! An excellent idea!

FRED. I volunteer—

TOPPER. No, no. Quite all right, Freddy, *I* volunteer. In fact, I insist. (MRS. FRED *nods her head in agreement.*)

FRED. Oh. Your every wish, my dear Topper. (*Searching his pockets.*) Now, where is that blasted handkerchief? (*From somewhere on its person,* CHRISTMAS PRESENT *produces a handkerchief—the one* DICKENS *gave* FORSTER— *and tosses it to* FRED.) Ah, here it is. (*He blindfolds* TOPPER.) Any last requests?

TOPPER. (*Looking in* MRS. FRED'S SISTER'S *direction.*) Only one. (*She giggles.*)

FRED. Here we go. One . . . (*He spins* TOPPER *around.*) Two . . . (*Spinning him around again.*) Three . . .

(*Spinning him for a final time, and with a shove, sending him in the direction of* MRS. FRED'S SISTER. *There is obviously collusion, here:* FRED, MRS. FRED, *and* TOPPER *try their best to corner* MRS. FRED'S SISTER *for*

TOPPER. FRED *produces a little bell, which he constantly rings above* MRS. FRED'S SISTER's *head—much to her annoyance.* TOPPER *makes feints at catching* FRED *and* MRS. FRED, *but they don't fool anyone. And, of course,* FRED *fixed the handkerchief so that* TOPPER *can see through it. As for* SCROOGE, *his icy spirit melts bit by bit, as the spirit grows contagious. He laughs, shouts warnings, and is entirely caught up in the whole thing. The game finally ends with* TOPPER *wrapping his arms around* MRS. FRED'S SISTER.)

TOPPER. Who could this be? (*He removes the handkerchief.*) Well, well, well. I really had no idea. I thought it was dear old Mrs. Fred.

SCROOGE. No he didn't, Spirit, no he didn't! He knew who it was all along. (*To* TOPPER.) Cheater!

FRED. Another game!

MRS. FRED. Another? Let's sit down. (*She does.*)

FRED. A word game, then.

CHRISTMAS PRESENT. My time grows short.

SCROOGE. But there's another game, Spirit. One more game.

CHRISTMAS PRESENT. If you wish. You may not find this one as amusing.

FRED. (*As the others sit around him.*) This game is called "Yes and No." I think of something, and you have to guess what it is by asking me questions which I can answer either "yes" or "no." (*A pause, as he thinks of a subject. As the game develops, and as they get closer to finding the answer,* FRED *has greater and greater difficulty supressing his laughter.*) All right. I've got it.

TOPPER. What is it?(*Thev laugh.*)

MRS. FRED. Is it a living thing?

FRED. Yes.

TOPPER. Is it an animal?

FRED. Yes.

MRS. FRED'S SISTER. Is it a tame animal?

FRED. No. It is rather disagreeable.

MRS. FRED. Is it savage, then?

FRED. Yes, fierce.

TOPPER. Does it make a noise?

FRED. Yes.

MRS. FRED'S SISTER. Does it bark?

FRED. In my opinion, no. Though some may differ on that point.

MRS. FRED. Does it meow?

FRED. Definitely not.

SCROOGE. That rules out the cats!

TOPPER. Does it howl?

FRED. No, not its style.

MRS. FRED. Does it growl?

MRS. FRED'S SISTER. Or grunt?

FRED. Yes. I'd say it does both. (*A pause, as they puzzle this out.*)

SCROOGE. He's got 'em stumped! A brilliant boy, Fred!

MRS. FRED. Is it a bear?

FRED. No.

MRS. FRED'S SISTER. Does it live in the jungle?

FRED. No.

TOPPER. Does it live in the zoo?

FRED. No. At least *I* don't think of it as a zoo.

MRS. FRED'S SISTER. (*To* MRS. FRED.) What does that mean? *He* doesn't think of it as a zoo?

TOPPER. (*Catching on.*) It must be a city, then. Does it live in a city?

FRED. Yes.

SCROOGE. Clever boy! But not clever enough for my Fred. That boy's as sharp as a needle!

TOPPER. Is it London?

FRED. Yes.

MRS. FRED. Does it walk the streets?

FRED. Yes.

MRS. FRED'S SISTER. Does anyone lead it?

FRED. Not that I've ever known. Heavens, no.

SCROOGE. Not a dog or a horse, then. Is it a person?

TOPPER. Is it sold in a market?

FRED. No. But it's often found near the Exchange.

MRS. FRED'S SISTER. What sort of animal is found near the Exchange?

MRS. FRED. Is it a sociable creature?

FRED. Most unsociable.

TOPPER. Does it live among others of its kind?

FRED. It positively despises its kind.

MRS. FRED'S SISTER. Is it an ass?

SCROOGE. (*While* FRED *ponders this, the laughter leaking out of him.*) How can it be an ass, you goose? An ass is led!

FRED. Nnnnnno.

MRS. FRED'S SISTER. (*Adding it up.*) It grunts and growls, lives in London, walks the streets . . . is disagreeable and unsociable . . . (*It suddenly strikes her. Like* FRED, *who can barely suppress it, she bursts into laughter.*)

SCROOGE. I know it! I know it!

MRS. FRED'S SISTER. I've found it out! I know what it is, Fred! I know what it is!

SCROOGE. (*Triumphantly, while* MRS. FRED'S SISTER *is still laughing helplessly.*) It's the tax collector!

MRS. FRED'S SISTER. It's your uncle Scroooooge!

(SCROOGE *is struck speechless. The others dissolve into laughter and applause.*)

TOPPER. Well, if that's the case, then your reply to the question, "Is it a bear?" ought to have been yes.

FRED. But he's not a bear.

TOPPER. No, but your negative answer was sufficient to divert our attention from him.

FRED. He's given us plenty of merriment, I'm sure, and it would be ungrateful not to drink his health. I say, "Uncle Scrooge!"

THE OTHERS. Uncle Scrooge! (*They drink.*)

CHRISTMAS PRESENT. (*To* SCROOGE.) You seem to be the source of much merriment.

SCROOGE. Yes, for others. (*Scrutinizing the* GHOST.) Your hair is grey, Spirit. Are spirits' lives so brief?

CHRISTMAS PRESENT. My life upon this globe is very short. It ends tonight.

SCROOGE. Tonight?

CHRISTMAS PRESENT. At midnight. The time grows near.

(*The party disappears.* [SOUND EFFECT #8: Tolling bells. First, just one, then, two, tolling twelve; wind and thunder crashes.] SCROOGE *and* CHRISTMAS PRESENT *are alone.*)

SCROOGE. What place is this?

CHRISTMAS PRESENT. Children are buried here.

SCROOGE. Children? (*The bells build.*)

CHRISTMAS PRESENT. It is the primary requirement for admittance that they be under the age of ten.

SCROOGE. Of what did these children die? (*The bells build.*)

CHRISTMAS PRESENT. Off too cruel a contact with the world. Of cold. Of disease. Of poverty. Of hunger. Of the ruthless neglect of comfortable thousands.

SCROOGE. They are buried so closely. They are almost one on top of the other. (*The bells continue to build.*)

CHRISTMAS PRESENT. A natural occurrence when their numbers are so great, and each child so small.

SCROOGE. But where did all these children come from, that they should end so soon?

CHRISTMAS PRESENT. Are there no prisons? Are there no workhouses? (*The* GHOST *begins backing Up Right, until he is out of sight.*)

SCROOGE. (*Over loud sounds of wind and chains.*) Spirit! Don't leave me in this place! (*The sound effect climaxes with a tremendous rolling thunder clap. The Upstage win-*

dow flies open, and there stands THE GHOST OF CHRISTMAS YET TO COME, *in the robe worn by* DICKENS *at the beginning of Act One. The hood is pulled over his face, and one arm is outstretched, accusingly, at* SCROOGE. *The* GHOST *is played by* FREDERICK. SCROOGE *falls to his knees.*) I am in the presence of the Ghost of Christmas Yet to Come? (*The* GHOST *nods.*) You are about to show me shadows of the things that have not yet happened, but will happen in the time before us. Is that so, Spirit? (*Again, just a nod. But* SCROOGE *cannot help but sense two eyes fixed upon him from deep within the shroud.*) Ghost of the future, I fear you more than any spectre I have seen. But as I know your purpose is to do me good, and as I hope to live to be another man from what I was, I am prepared to bear you company. (*A pause, as he waits for some kind of reply.*) Will you not speak to me? (*Again, nothing: just the arm, outstretched.*) Lead on. The night is waning fast, and it is precious time to me, I know. Lead on!

([SOUND EFFECT #9: A loud thunder crash.] *Lights come up, and three business men, each with a newspaper, enter. They are:* LEMON *as the* FAT MAN, FORSTER *as the* MAN WITH THE HANDKERCHIEF, *and* STANFIELD *as the* THIN MAN. *The* MAN WITH THE HANDKERCHIEF *has a rather severe head cold. They read their papers as they speak, with an occasional break to exchange a look, or a malicious giggle.*)

MAN WITH THE HANDKERCHIEF. (*Wiping his nose.*) Have you heard the news?

FAT MAN. Indeed I have.

THIN MAN. Do you know the details?

FAT MAN. No, I don't know much about it either way. I only know he's dead.

MAN WITH THE HANDKERCHIEF. When did he die?

FAT MAN. Last night, I believe.

THIN MAN. Why, whatever was the matter with him? I thought he'd never die.

MAN WITH THE HANDKERCHIEF. God knows.

THIN MAN. (*A most significant question.*) What has he done with his money? (*A pause.*)

FAT MAN. I haven't heard. Left it to his company, perhaps. He hasn't left it to me, that's all I know. (*They laugh.*) It's likely to be a very small funeral, for, upon my life, I don't know of anybody going to it. Suppose we make up a party, and volunteer? (*They exchange glances, and laugh.*)

MAN WITH THE HANDKERCHIEF. I don't mind going—if a lunch is provided. I'll make the pilgrimage, but I must be fed. (*Another laugh.*)

THIN MAN. Well, I am the most disinterested among you, for I never attend funerals, and I never eat lunch. But I'll offer to go if anybody else will. Come to think of it, I'm not sure I wasn't his most particular friend: we used to stop and speak whenever we met. (*Checking his watch.*) Bye-bye. Don't want to miss the morning's trading. (*He wanders off.*)

FAT MAN. No, no.

(*He and the* MAN WITH THE HANDKERCHIEF *turn aside in private conversation of a business nature, and exit.*)

SCROOGE. (*He speaks to the* GHOST, *but his eyes are scanning the Exchange all the while. Thus, he does not notice that the* GHOST *has momentarily vanished.*) Why, Spirit, this is the Exchange. And these are men of business —very wealthy and very important. They are my very good friends, for I always make a point of standing well in their esteem. (*A pause.*) But if this is the Exchange, and these are my associates, then where am I? I don't seem to be standing in my usual corner. And this is most certainly my time of day. (*Thinking he has found the answer.*) Spirit, I have been revolving in my mind a change of life. Could this be the outcome?

([SOUND EFFECT #10: wind, chains, and thunder.] *The lights dim.* LEMON *enters, lays on the chaise longue, and covers himself with a sheet.* CATHERINE *enters as* MRS. DILBER, *the laundress. She's a withered old woman, arms cramped with rheumatism and arthritis. She wears the old bonnet and ragged wig* DICKENS *gave her at the outset. She carries* SCROOGE'S *coat, in which are wrapped a pair of boots and a pair of spoons. She enters quickly, warily, running to the turret. She's looking for someone, who evidently is not there.*)

MRS. DILBER. (*Disappointed.*) Garn.

(*She turns to skulk off, and runs into* MRS. STANFIELD *as the* CHARWOMAN. *She, too, is an old, ratty grotesque, carrying a bed coverlet, in which is wrapped a white shirt. They collide, and frightened, scurry Off:* MRS. DILBER *against the turret, and the* CHARWOMAN *Downstage. They stand, realizing who the other is. Pawning the stolen property of a dead man is against the law, and the penalties are heavy.* STANFIELD *enters, wearing* FREDERICK'S *top hat, around which is tied* FORSTER'S *handkerchief: he is now the* UNDER-TAKER. *In his pockets, he carries a quill and an ink pot; in the hat, a pair of candlesticks. He freezes, on seeing the two women, before recognizing them. A moment of stand-off. Then, all three rush to the turret steps in an effort to be first in line. There is much pushing and shoving and hair-pulling, along with growls and hisses less than human. They retreat, licking their wounds.*)

CHARWOMAN. Let the charwoman alone be first. Let the laundress alone be second, and let the undertaker be third.

(*A pause, as the proposition is thought over. Then, another mad rush to the stairs.* OLD JOE, *the proprietor, enters Up Right and observes the melee.* CHRISTMAS YET TO COME *has re-entered, played now by* FORSTER—*because* OLD JOE, *a scruffy old gent with a broken top hat and an eye patch, is played by* FREDERICK.)

OLD JOE. Ay! (*The three customers halt and turn around.*)

MRS. DILBER. Look here Old Joe, here's a chance—if we haven't all three met here without meaning it.

OLD JOE. (*Climbing the turret steps as the others part with great deference. He sits on the high stool and sets down a large booty bag which he's brought on with him.*) You couldn't have met in a better place. We're all suited to our calling. We're well-matched. (*The* CHARWOMAN *opens the coverlet, and lays out her haul for inspection.*)

CHARWOMAN. (*Noticing that the other two are not displaying their take.*) What odds then? What odds, Mrs. Dilber? Every person has a right to take care of himself. *He* always did.

MRS. DILBER. That's true indeed. No man moreso.

CHARWOMAN. Why then, don't stand staring as if you was afraid, woman. Who's the wiser? We're not going to pick holes in each other's coats, I suppose?

MRS. DILBER. No, indeed. (*She unrolls the coat on the floor, and separates the boots and spoons.*)

UNDERTAKER. I should hope not.

CHARWOMAN. Very well, then, that's enough. Who's the worse for the loss of a few things like these? Not a dead man, I suppose.

MRS. DILBER. Not him.

UNDERTAKER. True enough. If he wanted to dispose of'em after he was dead, why wasn't he natural in his lifetime? If he had been, he'd have had somebody to look after him when he was struck with death, instead of gasping out his last there, alone.

MRS. DILBER. It's the truest word was ever spoke. It's a judgement on him, the wicked old screw.

CHARWOMAN. I wish it were a little heavier one. And it would have been, too, if I could have laid me hands on anything else. (*To* OLD JOE.) Examine that bundle, Joe, and let me know the value of it. Speak out plain. I'm not afraid to be the first, nor afraid for them to see it. We knew pretty well that we were helping ourselves before we met here, I believe. It's no sin. Examine the bundle, Joe.

UNDERTAKER. (*Grabbing her by the hair, and forcefully sitting her down.*) No my dear, you mustn't. (*To* OLD JOE.) Joe, appraise my lot first.

CHARWOMAN. (*Rubbing her neck.*) That's what I've admired in you all these years—always the gentleman.

(*The* UNDERTAKER *produces the quill and ink pot, and hands them over to* OLD JOE, *who examines them carefully, and, with little more than a grunt, puts them in his sack. The* UNDERTAKER *hands him the candlesticks.*)

OLD JOE. (*Examining them critically, holding them up to the light.*) Hmmm . . . umph . . . well, these are originals. Haven't seen their like in at least an half-an-hour. (*He laughs, and so do the* CHARWOMAN *and* MRS. DILBER, *delighting in the* UNDERTAKER'S *meager haul.* OLD JOE *drops a few coins into the* UNDERTAKER'S *hand.*) That's your account, and I wouldn't give another sixpence if I was to be boiled for not doing it.

UNDERTAKER. (*Outraged, he raises his fist.*) Why—

OLD JOE. (*Standing.*) Don't try nothing, old man.

(*Furious, the* UNDERTAKER *spits on* MRS. DILBER, *and the* CHARWOMAN, *who are still laughing. Angrily, he exits.*)

OLD JOE. (*Sitting.*) Who's next?

MRS. DILBER. (*Pushing the* CHARWOMAN *aside, as she stands.*) I'll be next. (*She hands* OLD JOE *the spoons. He looks them over.*) Them's nice items, barely used. Don't suppose he ate off 'em much. Probably thought they was too valuable to wear out rubbing against his tongue!

OLD JOE. (*Paying her.*) Two shillings.

MRS. DILBER. Worth twice that much.

OLD JOE. (*Examining the boots.*) Now, these ain't bad. Rather handsome. (*Testing the thickness of the souls.*) A mite thin, though. Four shillings. (*He puts them in the pag, and pays her.*)

MRS. DILBER. I'd pay a high price for them boots. Boots is precious, these days.

OLD JOE. Have pity on me, Mrs. Dilber. I'm just a poor old man trying to survive me retirement. (*He picks up the coat, searching for holes and weak seams.*) Sturdy. Could last another winter. (*Considering.*) But it ain't the style. Have to knock off for that.

MRS. DILBER. (*Disgusted.*) What yer being so pinchfisted about? Yer a regular miser, as bad as he. No one cares a penny for the style.

OLD JOE. (*Genially, as he stuffs the coat in the bag.*) I always gives to much to the ladies. It's a weakness of mine, and that's the way I'll ruin meself. (*Less genially, as he pays her.*) And if you ask me for another penny, I'll repent of being so liberal, and knock off half-a-crown.

(*Angrily, she grabs the money and leaves. Almost Off, she turns, as if to speak.* OLD JOE *tips his hat and smiles. Thinking better of it, she says nothing, and exits.*)

CHARWOMAN. (*With confidence.*) Examine me bundle, Joe.

OLD JOE. (*Coming down off the turret, and down to the* CHARWOMAN's *loot, he holds up the coverlet.*) What do you call this? His coverlet?

CHARWOMAN. (*Great pride.*) His coverlet!

OLD JOE. You don't mean to say you took it right off him—with him laying there?

CHARWOMAN. I do. Why not?

OLD JOE. (*Appreciating a fellow professional.*) You were born to make yer fortune, and you'll certainly do it.

CHARWOMAN. I shan't hold my hand when I can get anything in it by reaching out—especially for the sake of such a man as he was, I promise you. He ain't likely to take cold without it, I daresay.

OLD JOE. (*Suddenly doubtful.*) I hope he didn't die of anything catching, eh? (*He drops it and picks up the shirt.*)

CHARWOMAN. Don't be afraid of that. I ain't so fond of his company that I'd loiter about him if he did. You can look through that shirt til yer eyes fall out, but you won't find a hole in it or a threadbare place. Best he had, and a fine one, too. They'd have wasted it if it hadn't been for me.

OLD JOE. What do you call wasting it?

CHARWOMAN. Putting it on him to be buried in. Somebody was fool enough to do it, but I took it off again. If calico ain't good enough for such a purpose, it ain't good for anything. It's quite as becoming to the body. He can't look any uglier than he did in that one.

OLD JOE. Yer a rare one. A rare one! (*He stuffs them in the bag, and pays her. Meanwhile, she produces a crumpled piece of paper from her dress.* JOE *takes it.*) Now, what's this?

CHARWOMAN. (*As he unwraps it.*) That's the prize of it all, that is. Wrapped in a piece of paper, under a pile of old ledgers in the bottom of a trunk.

OLD JOE. (*Carefully holding it up to the light—it's the ring.*) I wonder what he was doing with such a thing. (*Chuckling.*) Think he was going to give it to some lady?

CHARWOMAN. None in their proper minds would have such a one as he was. He was just like the undertaker said: unnatural, from first to last.

OLD JOE. (*Greatly excited over such a valuable find.*) A valuable piece. It'll fetch a nice price and feed old Joseph for a month. (*He pays her for the ring, and puts it on his little finger.*)

CHARWOMAN. This is the end of it, you see. He frightened everyone away from him while he was alive, to profit us when he was dead! (*They both laugh, and steal away.*)

SCROOGE. Spirit, I see, I see. The case of this unhappy man might be my own. It tends that way now. ([SOUND EFFECT #11: Thunder, wind, and chains.] *Recoiling from the scene,* SCROOGE *turns upon the sheeted figure on the bed.*) Merciful heavens, what is this! (*The* GHOST *points toward the bed.*) Is this the man, Spirit, whose belongings these scavengers have plundered? (*The* GHOST *responds by pointing to the head beneath the sheet.* SCROOGE *understands what is being asked of him.*) Spirit, this is a fearful place. In leaving it, I shall not leave its lesson, trust me. Let us go. (*Still, the* GHOST *points with an unmoving finger toward the head.*) I understand you, and would do it if I could. But I have not the power, Spirit. I have not the power! Surely there is one man or woman or child who will speak kindly of him? Show me that person, Spirit, I beseech you! (*A pause.*) Let me see then *some* tenderness connected with a death, or this dark chamber will be forever present to me.

([SOUND EFFECT #12: Thunder, wind, and chains.] *Under the sound effect, the* CRATCHIT *house is set up again. The family is quiet:* PETER *sits near the table reading;* MARTHA *is setting the table, and then will stir the punch;* MRS. CRATCHIT *sits by the fire sewing, and* BELINDA *is near her, spooling yearn. By the chimney is the small stool and the crutch.*)

MRS. CRATCHIT. (*Putting her sewing down, and wiping*

her eyes. To MARTHA, *who notices.*) The light hurts my eyes. (*A pause. Apologetically.*) It makes them weak, working by candlelight. For the world, I wouldn't show weak eyes to your father when he comes home. It must be near his time.

PETER. Past it, rather. But I think he's walked a little slower these past few nights.

MRS. CRATCHIT. With Tim on his shoulder, he used to walk very fast indeed.

PETER. I've known him to run, nearly.

BELINDA. He galloped. (*A pause.*)

MRS. CRATCHIT. But he was very light to carry. And your father loved him so that it was no bother. (*A sound on the stairs.*) There's your father at the door. (CRATCHIT *enters;* MRS. CRATCHIT *goes to greet him.*)

CRATCHIT. Merry Christmas, my dear.

MRS. CRATCHIT. Merry Christmas.

CRATCHIT. (*Hanging up his comforter.*) The goose smells delicious. And the pudding—I think I can taste it already. Did you help your mother, Belinda?

MRS. CRATCHIT. She made the pudding.

BELINDA. By myself, I did.

CRATCHIT. No! You'll have your own bakery shop before you know it.

MRS. CRATCHIT. You were gone a long time, Bob.

CRATCHIT. (*Coming down the steps into the room.*) Yes, I took a longer way. (*A pause.*)

MRS. CRATCHIT. You went today, then?

CRATCHIT. Yes, my dear. I wish you could have gone. It would have done you good to see how green a place it is, even this time of year. I promised him we'd walk there often, of a Sunday.

MRS. CRATCHIT. I'll go soon. When the weather warms.

CRATCHIT. I should be making my punch.

MARTHA. It's already made, father. I wanted to save you the trouble.

CRATCHIT. (*Going to the table. He puts on a cheerful expression, as he pours the punch and passes it around the table.*) It's no trouble. It's always one of my greatest pleasures this time of year. And this is the best time of year, I believe. Am I right? (*No reply from the family.*) Am I right, Peter?

PETER. Yes.

CRATCHIT. Of course. (*Straining a bit more.*) You'll never guess who I met on the street today. Mister Scrooge's nephew. He only sees me once a year, you know. Yet he talked as if we were the oldest of friends, and on the most intimate terms. He'd heard about our—distress—and he said, "I'm mighty sorry for it, Mister Cratchit. And heartily sorry for your good wife." By the bye, how he knew *that*, I don't know.

MRS. CRATCHIT. Knew what, dear?

CRATCHIT. Why, that you're a good wife.

PETER. Everybody knows that.

CRATCHIT. Very well observed, my boy! I hope they do. "Heartily sorry," he said, "for your good wife." (*A pause.*) Now, gather 'round for a toast. (*The family gathers round him, and they raise their mugs.*) A merry Christmas to us all . . . And a healthy New . . . (*His voice breaks, and he lowers his mug. The family holds him.*) My little boy . . . my poor little boy . . .

SCROOGE. (*He would protest more vigorously if he had the spirit.*) Spirit, tell me: is there a reason the boy had to die? (*Nothing from the* GHOST.) I know not how, but something informs me that our parting moment is at hand. Tell me . . . what man was that whom we saw lying dead? ([SOUND EFFECT #13: Tolling bells, thunder, and wind.] *Grows progressively louder as the scene goes on. The lights grow dim, and the* CRATCHITS *vanish.* STANFIELD *and* FREDERICK *cross Down Left on the first level, behind the trunk. They crouch behind it.*) A church yard? (*The* GHOST *points towards the trunk.*) Before I draw nearer, answer me one question. Are these the shadows of things that *will* be, or are they the shadows of things that *may* be, only? (*No answer from the* GHOST. *A second bell begins to chime.*) Spirit, hear me. I am not the man I was. I will not be the man I have been. Why show me this if I am past all hope? (*Loud thunder crash.*) Good Spirit, you pity me. (*Another loud crash of thunder, as* STANFIELD *and* FREDERICK *lift the trunk up on end, to reveal, on the trunk's bottom, a gravestone, reading "Ebenezer Scrooge RIP."* SCROOGE *falls to his knees in horror.*) No, Spirit, no! (*The* GHOST *begins backing out Up Right.*) I will honor Christmas in my heart, and try to keep it all the year. I will live in the past, the present, and the future. The Spirits of all three shall strive within me. I will not shut out the lessons that they teach. Tell me Spirit that I may sponge away the writing on this stone! (*He pulls the stone over; the trunk falls with a crash. He follows the* GHOST *to the Up Right door, and grabs it to beseech it—and comes away with an empty cloak. He wrestles in its folds, and falls into bed, as:* [SOUND EFFECT #14: Tower chimes tolling five.] SCROOGE *wrestles with the cloak in bed, as the stage grows brighter.*) I will live in the past, the present, and the future . . . the past, the present, and the future . . . the past, the present . . . (*A pause. He awakes, taking a moment to realise where he is.*) I'm alive . . . (*Feeling himself, to make sure.*) I'm alive . . . (*Taking in the room.*) and this bed is my own. And this room is my own . . . And the time before me is my own. The Ghost spared me! I knew it! (*He jumps up on his feet, opening the Downstage window.*) I *will* live in the past, the present, and the future! The spirits of all three *shall* strive within me! Oh, Jacob Marley! Heaven and Christmas time be praised for this! I say it on my knees, old Jacob. (*He's on his knees.*) On my knees! (*He's up again, carreening about the room.*) I don't know what to do! I'm as light as a feather! I'm as happy as an angel! I'm as merry as a schoolboy! I'm as giddy as a drunken man! (*He wheels about, taking in the entire room.*) There's the saucepan that the gruel was in . . . there's the door by which the ghost of Jacob Marley entered . . . there's the corner where the Ghost of Christmas Present sat! It's all right, it's all true, it all happened! (*He leaps onto the bed.*) A merry Christmas to everybody! A happy New Year to all the world! (*He's off the bed again.*) I don't know what day of the month it is. I don't know how long I've been among the spirits. I don't know anything. I'm quite a baby! Never mind, I don't care. I'd rather be a baby! (*Opening the Upstage window.*) Hello! Whoop! (SOUND EFFECT #15: A cacophony of bells.) Glorious! Glorious! (CHARLEY *enters as a street boy. He pauses, hurls a snowball at an Offstage assailant, and does a somersault Downstage. To* CHARLEY.) Hello there! Hello! What's today?

BOY. (*Tying a shoe lace.*) Eh?

SCROOGE. What's today, my fine fellow?

BOY. (*How could anyone not know?*) Today? Why, it's Christmas Day!

SCROOGE. It's Christmas Day! I haven't missed it! The spirits have done it all in one night. They can do anything they like. Of course they can! Hello there, my fine fellow!

BOY. (*Trying to figure this strange bird out.*) Hello.

SCROOGE. Do you know the poulterer's, in the next street but one? The one at the corner?

BOY. I should hope I did.

SCROOGE. An intelligent boy! A remarkable boy! Do you know whether they've sold the prize turkey that was hanging there? Not the little prize turkey—the big one?

BOY. What, the one as big as me?

SCROOGE. What a delightful boy! It's a pleasure to talk with him. Yes, my buck!

BOY. It's hanging there now.

SCROOGE. Is it? Go buy it!

BOY. Buy it yourself!

SCROOGE. No, no, I'm serious. Go and buy it, and tell

'em to bring it here that I may give 'em direction where to take it. Come back with the man and I'll give you a shilling! (*The* BOY *turns to run off.*) Come back with him in less than five minutes, and I'll give you half-a-crown!

BOY. Garn! (*He runs off to fetch the poulterer.*)

SCROOGE. I'll send it to Bob Cratchit's. He shan't know who sent it. It's twice the size of Tiny Tim! Four times the size of Tiny Tim!

(*He takes off the night cap and sleeping gown, and struggles into his coat. He is now out in the street. The two* PORTLY GENTLEMEN *enter Up Right, crossing Down.*)

FIRST PORTLY GENTLEMAN. (*Recognizing* SCROOGE, *he tries to sidestep him and continue on his way.*) Scrooge and Marley's, I believe?

SCROOGE. (*Stopping them and pumping their hands.*) My dear sirs, how do you do? I hope you succeeded yesterday. It was very kind of you—a wonderful gesture. A merry Christmas to you both!

FIRST PORTLY GENTLEMAN. Mister Scrooge?

SCROOGE. Yes, that is my name, and I fear it may not be very pleasant to you. Allow me to ask your pardon. And will you have the goodness—(*He whispers into the* FIRST PORTLY GENTLEMAN'S *ear the size of the contribution he wishes to make.*)

FIRST PORTLY GENTLEMAN. Lord bless me! (*He whispers it to the* SECOND PORTLY GENTLEMAN, *who gasps, and takes out his handkerchief to mop his brow.*) My dear Mister Scrooge, are you serious?

SCROOGE. If you please. Not a farthing less. A great many back-payments are included in it, I assure you. Will you do me that favor?

SECOND PORTLY GENTLEMAN. My dear Sir, I don't know what to say to such munificence—

SCROOGE. Don't say anything! Come and see me. Will you come and see me?

FIRST PORTLY GENTLEMAN. I will!

SECOND PORTLY GENTLEMAN. And *I* will! We *both* will!

SCROOGE. Thank'ee. I'm much obliged to you. I thank you fifty times! Bless you!

(*The two* PORTLY GENTLEMEN *are off—or they may take seats to watch the action, as* LEMON *and* FORSTER.)

DICKENS. Scrooge went to church, and walked about the streets, and patted the children on the head. He had never dreamed that anything could give him so much happiness. In the afternoon, he turned his steps towards his nephew's house. He passed the door a dozen times before he had the courage to go up and knock.

(*He exits through the Up Right door. A brief pause. Then he knocks.* FREDERICK *enters through the door on the turret as* FRED. *He crosses Down and opens the door— confronted by a meek* SCROOGE.)

SCROOGE. Fred . . . (*A pause, as* FRED *must look twice.*)

FRED. Uncle Scrooge? (*Another brief pause.*) It's Uncle Scrooge! (*He runs toward the turret with the news.*) It's Uncle Scrooge!

(*He runs back to bring* SCROOGE *inside.* MRS. FRED, TOPPER, *and* MRS. FRED'S SISTER *enter.* DICKENS *greets each one as he mentions their names—and pulls a carrot from his pocket, and holds it to his nose— delighting the group.*)

DICKENS. Let him in? It's a mercy he didn't shake his arm off. He was at home in five minutes. His niece looked just the same, so did Topper, so did the sister. Wonderful party, wonderful games, wonderful unanimity, wonderful happiness! (*Quickly he moves on, setting up* SCROOGE's *office, with* FORSTER's *help. This time, they place the desk and chair Downstage on the second level, facing the Up Right door.*) But he was early at the office next morning. If he could only be there first, and catch Bob Cratchit coming late. That was the thing he had his heart set upon. (*He sits in* SCROOGE's *chair.* MRS. STANFIELD *rings the hand bell nine times.*) The clock struck nine. No Bob. A quarter past. No Bob. He was a full eighteen minutes behind his time.

(CRATCHIT *rushes in with the intent of hurrying to his desk—but is stopped cold at the sight of* SCROOGE *waiting for him.*)

CRATCHIT. Good morning, Mister Scrooge.

SCROOGE. (*Feigning his old scowl as best he can.*) "Good morning, Mister Scrooge." What do you mean by coming in here this time of day?

CRATCHIT. I am very sorry, Sir. I *am* a bit behind my time.

SCROOGE. I should say you are. Step this way, Sir, if you please.

CRATCHIT. (*Approaching* SCROOGE.) It's only once a year, Sir. It shan't be repeated. I was making rather merry yesterday, Sir . . .

SCROOGE. (*Grasping him by his comforter.*) Now I'll tell you what, my friend. I am not going to stand for this sort of thing any longer—

CRATCHIT. Mister Scrooge, I—

SCROOGE. And therefore . . . (*A pause.*) and therefore . . . I am about to raise your salary! (*Another pause, as* SCROOGE *lets him go.* CRATCHIT *just stands there, stunned.*) A merry Christmas, Bob! A merrier Christmas, Bob my good fellow, than I have given you for many a year! (CRATCHIT *recovers, and dashes for the fireplace, where he picks up the stool, to defend himself from this madman.*) I'll raise your salary, and endeavor to assist your family, and we'll discuss your affairs this very afternoon, over a Christmas bowl of your special punch. (*Seeing that* SCROOGE *is evidently in earnest,* CRATCHIT *has put the stool down.*) Make up the fire, and buy another coal-scuttle before you dot another i, Bob Cratchit! (*Digging into his pocket, he pulls out some coins and presses them into* CRATCHIT's *hand.*)

CRATCHIT. Yes, sir. Thank you, sir. (*A pause.*) And a Merry Christmas . . . Mister Scrooge. (*He exits.*)

SCROOGE. (*Coming Downstage.*) Oh, Jacob Marley, I shall remember you as long as I live. A wonderful gift! A merry Christmas, Jacob . . . wherever you are.

(*A pause.* DICKENS *removes the wig, nose, and glasses. He takes off the coat and hangs it over the back of the chair. He crosses to* HELEN *and* CHARLEY, *and brings them Downstage.*)

DICKENS. Scrooge was better than his word. He did it all and infinitely more. And to Tiny Tim, who did *not* die, he was a second father. He became as good a friend, as good a master, and as good a man as the good old city knew. Some people laughed to see the alteration in him, but he let them laugh, and paid them little heed. For he was wise enough to know that nothing ever happens for good on this globe at which some people do not have their fill of laughter at the outset. His own heart laughed, and that was quite enough for him. He had no further intercourse with spirits, but lived upon the Total Abstinence Principle ever afterwards. And it was always said of him that he knew how to keep Christmas well, if any man alive possessed the knowledge. And, I might add, Scrooge never again attempted to forget his past, nor make an orphan of it. Instead, he gained from its lessons, and made it a part of him. For it occured to him that his maker—and ours, too—gave him a memory with a very specific purpose in mind.

LEMON. Speaking of memory, I recall there being a

large goose in the oven downstairs. Are we going to eat it or aren't we?

DICKENS. Directly.

CHARLEY. (*To* DICKENS, *after some prompting from* CATHERINE.) Are you going to write this story down?

DICKENS. Well, Charley, that may be a good idea. We can't have these lavish parties for the sake of Uncle Porpoise's stomach without the means to furnish the goose and the dressing, can we?

CHARLEY. (*Presenting* DICKENS *with a gift, wrapped in cloth.*) Then you'll need these.

DICKENS. (*Inspecting it delightedly.*) What is it? (*Shaking it.*) Not a clock, I'll be bound. (*He opens it. It is, in fact, a pair of quill pens.*)

CHARLEY. Merry Christmas.

DICKENS. Thank you, Charley. (*A pause.*) Never fear, Uncle Porpoise! Next year's gathering is assured!

CATHERINE. Let's attend to this year's gathering first. And, as Mary's gone home, we're going to need some assistance.

LEMON. Helen and I will check the goose.

HELEN. (*As in the* CRATCHIT *scene.*) We mustn't let it get overdone.

LEMON. What if it were! Run, Helen! (*They exit.*)

FORSTER. I'd better go behind and give him a push, in case he gets jammed in the stairwell. (*He exits.*)

DICKENS. Help the ladies with the punch bowl, will you Stanny?

STANFIELD. (*Going to assist* CATHERINE *and* MRS. STANFIELD, *who are gathering things up.*) Of course.

DICKENS. And Frederick, the glasses. Charley and I will put out the lights.

(*The next six lines are said as the room grows darker. The tail end of them come through the darkness. They all are exiting.*)

STANFIELD. You know, Freddy, I was impressed, over-all, by your performances. Except for a major flaw here and there in your characterizations, you really quite surprised me. (*To* MRS. STANFIELD.) Didn't he surprise you, my dear?

MRS. STANFIELD. (*Keeping up the joke.*) Oh, yes, I was very impressed. I never knew you were hiding so much talent.

CATHERINE. You'll get him going and he won't stop for hours.

FREDERICK. Yes, well, that's why you're just a painter, Stanny. The bulk of your talent has yet to find its way out of your right hand. I, contrarily . . . well, what more can be said . . . ?

STANFIELD. Very little, I'm sure . . .

(*They are off. Silence. Then:* [SOUND EFFECT #16: Big Ben tolling nine.] THE CHILD *appears. A pause, as* DICKENS *sees him.*)

THE CHILD. Merry Christmas. (*Another pause.*)

DICKENS. The same to you.

THE CHILD. I liked the story.

DICKENS. Thank you. I have an idea for another one. Would you like to hear it? (*They meet, and take hands.*)

THE CHILD. Does it have a boy in it?

DICKENS. Yes, but no crutch. (*They sit on the chair behind the desk,* THE CHILD *on* DICKENS's *lap.*) There are two children, a boy and his sister. And a sea captain and his mate. Now, the father of the children is a fellow named . . . oh, let's say, 'Dombey' . . . (*The lights fade, as he talks.*)

NOTE: In the original production, the entire cast sang a choral arrangement of "The Christmas Child" as a part of the curtain call. The arrangement is included with this script.

PROPERTY LIST

(It should be noted that several characters share props.)

PERSONAL PROPS:

DICKENS
branch from Christmas tree stuck in a small pot
sheet
coat rack which holds:
   small crutch
   boy's cap*
   shawl*
   bonnet with ragged grey wig attached*
   quill pen*
   top hat*
   Welsh wig*
   large colored handkerchief*
comforter (long woollen scarf)
gold engagement band (in vest pocket)
small scroll (in coat pocket)
keys on a string long enough to fit around his neck
carrot
coins

FREDERICK
horse collar with chains
candy cane or piece of fruit
small wrapped gift
pocket watch
2 or 3 apples and oranges
4 long carrots
booty bag
coins
book

* Each of these is tied with ribbon to a small scroll.

82

CATHERINE
punch bowl with punch
tray of old mugs and an old pitcher
table cloth
pair of boots (mens)
3 or 4 silver spoons
needle
thread
shirt for mending

STANFIELD
bowl of apples and oranges
newspaper
pocket watch
quill pen
ink pot
candle sticks

MRS. STANFIELD
tray of punch glasses
box of tinware
bed coverlet
white shirt

FORSTER
portly gentlemens' credentials
small notebook with pencil
calling card
doorknob
white wig and beard
newspaper

LEMON
hard candy
glass of punch
newspaper

CHARLEY
box of Christmas decorations
book

roast goose on platter
2 quill pens, wrapped as a gift

HELEN
box of Christmas decorations
pudding
2 candles in candlesticks
roll of yarn

STAGE PROPS

Coat Rack in Act Two Preset
long, dark green mantle

Trunk (Itself a prop)
toy drum and drumsticks
violin and bow
small crutch (later on DICKENS's coat rack)
ink pot
quill pen
money sacks with coins
coin holder with coins
wrapped Christmas gifts
piece of chalk

On Desk
candle
candlestick
matches
several pages of a manuscript
3 quill pens
ink pot

In Desk Drawer
stack of bills
make-up box with make-up
grey wig
spectacles
false nose

On Desk Chair
SCROOGE's coat

Mantlepiece
decanter
small hand bell (very light, tinkling tone)

By Fireplace
fire irons
wood box with wood
gruel pan and spoon

In Window Seat
nightgown
sleeping cap
shawl
quilt (On window seat in Act Two preset)

Beneath Chaise Longue
old wooden box containing:
    wooden soldier whose arms and legs move with the pull
      of a string
    tumbler who rolls about
    plaster of paris frog

Bookshelves
books

LITTLE CHRISTMAS CHILD
Act I dances

Michael Griffith

87

LITTLE CHRISTMAS CHILD

LITTLE CHRISTMAS CHILD
company version - for curtain calls

89

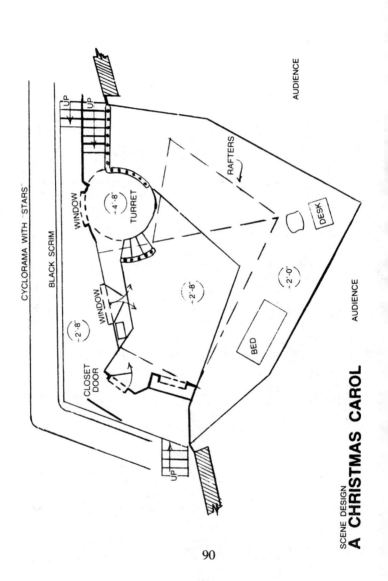

SCENE DESIGN
A CHRISTMAS CAROL

NEW

BROADWAY COMEDIES

from

SAMUEL FRENCH, INC.

DIVISION STREET – DOGG'S HAMLET,
CAHOOT'S MACBETH – FOOLS – GOREY
STORIES – GROWNUPS – I OUGHT TO BE IN
PICTURES – IT HAD TO BE YOU – JOHNNY
ON A SPOT – THE KINGFISHER – A LIFE –
LOOSE ENDS – LUNCH HOUR – MURDER AT
THE HOWARD JOHNSON'S – NIGHT AND DAY –
ONCE A CATHOLIC – ROMANTIC COMEDY –
ROSE – SPECIAL OCCASIONS – THE SUICIDE
– THE SUPPORTING CAST – WALLY'S CAFE

For descriptions of plays, consult our   Basic Catalogue of Plays.

New Broadway Hits

THE CURSE OF AN ACHING HEART • PAST TENSE
PUMP BOYS AND DINETTES • EMINENT DOMAIN
COME BACK TO THE 5 & DIME, JIMMY DEAN,
JIMMY DEAN
IT HAD TO BE YOU • WALLY'S CAFE
I WON'T DANCE • A LESSON FROM ALOES
I OUGHT TO BE IN PICTURES • THE KINGFISHER
FAITH HEALER • THE SUPPORTING CAST
MURDER AT THE HOWARD JOHNSON'S
LUNCH HOUR • HEARTLAND • GROWNUPS
ROMANTIC COMEDY • A TALENT FOR MURDER
HOROWITZ AND MRS. WASHINGTON • ROSE
SCENES AND REVELATIONS • DIVISION STREET
TO GRANDMOTHER'S HOUSE WE GO • TRIBUTE
NIGHT AND DAY • THE ELEPHANT MAN • DA
NUTS • WINGS • MORNING'S AT SEVEN
FOOLS • LOOSE ENDS • BENT • FILUMENA
THE DRESSER • BEYOND THERAPY
AMADEUS • ONCE A CATHOLIC

Information on Request

SAMUEL FRENCH, INC.

45 West 25th St.   NEW YORK 10010

6 RMS RIV VU
BOB RANDALL
(Little Theatre) Comedy
4 Men, 4 Women, Interior

A vacant apartment with a river view is open for inspection by prospective tenants, and among them are a man and a woman who have never met before. They are the last to leave and, when they get ready to depart, they find that the door is locked and they are shut in. Since they are attractive young people, they find each other interesting and the fact that both are happily married adds to their delight of mutual, yet obviously separate interests.

> ". . . a Broadway comedy of fun and class, as cheerful as a rising souffle. A sprightly, happy comedy of charm and humor. Two people playing out a very vital game of love, an attractive fantasy with a precious tincture of truth to it."—*N.Y. Times.*
> ". . . perfectly charming entertainment, sexy, romantic and funny."—*Women's Wear Daily.*

Royalty, $50–$35

WHO KILLED SANTA CLAUS?
TERENCE FEELY
(All Groups) Thriller
6 Men, 2 Women, Interior

Barbara Love is a popular television 'auntie'. It is Christmas, and a number of men connected with her are coming to a party. Her secretary, Connie, is also there. Before they arrive she is threatened by a disguised voice on her Ansaphone, and is sent a grotesque 'murdered' doll in a coffin, wearing a dress resembling one of her own. She calls the police, and a handsome detective arrives. Shortly afterwards her guests follow. It becomes apparent that one of those guests is planning to kill her. Or is it the strange young man who turns up unexpectedly, claiming to belong to the publicity department, but unknown to any of the others?

> ". . . is a thriller with heaps of suspense, surprises, and nattily cleaver turns and twists . . . Mr. Feeley is technically highly skilled in the artificial range of operations, and his dialogue is brilliantly effective."—The Stage. London.

Royalty, $50–$25

SAMUEL FRENCH has:

AMERICA'S
FAVORITE COMEDIES

THE MIND WITH THE DIRTY MAN – MOVE OVER,
MRS. MARKHAM – MURDER AT THE HOWARD
JOHNSON'S – MY DAUGHTER'S RATED "X" –
MY HUSBAND'S WILD DESIRES ALMOST DROVE ME
MAD – NATALIE NEEDS A NIGHTIE – NEVER
GET SMART WITH AN ANGEL – NEVER TOO LATE –
THE NORMAN CONQUESTS – NORMAN, IS THAT
YOU? – THE ODD COUPLE – THE OWL AND THE
PUSSYCAT – PLAY IT AGAIN, SAM – PLAZA SUITE –
THE PRISONER OF 2ND AVENUE – P.S., YOUR
CAT IS DEAD – THE RAINMAKER – ROMANTIC
COMEDY – SAME TIME, NEXT YEAR –
SAVE GRAND CENTRAL – SEE HOW THEY RUN
– SHRUNKEN HEADS – 6 RMS, RIV VU –
THE SQUARE ROOT OF LOVE – SUITEHEARTS –
THE SUNSHINE BOYS – TEN NIGHTS IN A BARROOM
– THERE'S A GIRL IN MY SOUP – 13 RUE DE
L'AMOUR – A THOUSAND CLOWNS – TWO FOR
THE SEASAW – VANITIES – WALLY'S CAFE

For descriptions of all plays, consult our   *Basic Catalogue of*
Plays.

HANDBOOK

for

THEATRICAL APPRENTICES

By Dorothy Lee Tompkins

Here is a common sense book on theatre, fittingly sub-titled, "A Practical Guide in All Phases of Theatre." Miss Tompkins has wisely left art to the artists and written a book which deals only with the practical side of the theatre. All the jobs of the theatre are categorized, from the star to the person who sells soft drinks at intermission. Each job is defined, and its basic responsibilities given in detail. An invaluable manual for every theatre group in explaining to novices the duties of apprenticeship, and in reassessing its own organizational structure and functions.

"If you are an apprentice or are just aspiring in any capacity, then you'll want to read and own Dorothy Lee Tompkins' A HANDBOOK FOR THEATRICAL APPRENTICES. It should be required reading for any drama student anywhere and is a natural for the amateur in any phase of the theatre."—George Freedley, Morning Telegraph.

"It would be helpful if the HANDBOOK FOR THE-ATRICAL APPRENTICES were in school or theatri-cal library to be used during each production as a guide to all participants."—Florence E. Hill, Dra-matics Magazine.